The Meat and Spirit Plan

A NOVEL

Selah
Saterstrom

COFFEE HOUSE PRESS

MINNEAPOLIS :: 2007

Coffee House Press books are available to the trade through our primary distributor, Consortium Book Sales & Distribution, www.cbsd.com or (800) 283-3572. For personal orders, catalogs, or other information, write to info@coffeehousepress.org.

Coffee House Press is a nonprofit literary publishing house. Support from private foundations, corporate giving programs, government programs, and generous individuals helps make the publication of our books possible. We gratefully acknowledge their support in detail in the back of this book.

Good books are brewing at coffeehousepress.org

LIBRARY OF CONGRESS CATALOGING-IN-PUBLICATION DATA
Saterstrom, Selah, 1974–
The Meat & spirit plan : a novel / by Selah Saterstrom.
p. cm.
ISBN-13: 978-1-56689-201-8 (alk. paper)
ISBN-10: 1-56689-201-5 (alk. paper)
1. Teenage girls—Fiction. 2. Southern States—Fiction.
I. Title. II. Title: Meat and spirit plan.
PS3619.A818M43 2007
813'.6—DC22
2007021002

ACKNOWLEDGMENTS
Grateful acknowledgments to the following publications, in which some of this work, in various forms, first appeared: *Tarpaulin Sky, Cranbrook Magazine, 14 Hills, Harness,* and *Sleepingfish.*

Ten percent of author proceeds from the sale of this book will go to Our Voice, a nonprofit crisis intervention agency serving Western North Carolina. An additional ten percent of proceeds will go toward the Kim Duckett Fund For Women.

For Noah, Lori, Brett,
and for my sister,
Kelly

Listen, Ginger Rogers loved feathers and wore sobs of them. Flesh wax, then ash. Listen, in some of those ovens there were birds made of folded paper. No one dared touch them. It was all there was and people feared touching them. Listen, on the way to the county fair there was an accident.

A girl walks a dirt road alone.

Then under a bridge, kid gloves made of pig. Mattress springs, pieces of airplane wreckage. Your ash, your head helmet wig of what was to come. So that many years later, a ritual, nocturne: Remove the straps.

Be naked. Paintings of devils, then devils themselves.

Headbanger's Ball

Hostage of This Nameless Feeling

Get Off Your High Horse and
Come to the Party

Make a Joke and I Will Sigh and
You Will Laugh and I Will Cry

This May Hurt a Little but It's
Something You'll Get Used To

Rock Hard, Ride Free

Run to the Hills, Run for Your Lives

From the Inside Out It All
Looks the Same

Darling, Do You Wear the Mark

Crazy but That's How It Goes

Master, Master Where's the Dreams
I've Been After

The Only Good Indians Are Tame

ISTEN, I AM IN LOVE. MY SISTER LOST HER virginity to Anthony Amara when she was fourteen and I plan on doing the same. If not with Anthony, with his cousin Claude. The Amara cousins tell me I will be beautiful. My sister pretends to be mad and threatens them. She is home from college and we are temporarily living in my grandmother's house for the summer while our grandmother rotates summer months between sisters. My sister has friends. They move in too. Everyone gets drunk at night. My sister does not allow me to drink more than one but I drink more than one after she is drunk then she thinks it is funny. One night Anthony cooks steaks. A big deal because steaks are expensive and not everyone knows how to cook them good. We eat in the living room and when people take plates to the kitchen Anthony and I remain. He picks up my foot and places it in his crotch. He moves the heel of my foot into it. I resist. He raises an eyebrow and asks if I masturbate. Every time I do not answer he digs my heel deeper. He says: I know you do. I finally tell him I know how. My sister walks into the room and he drops my foot to the hardwood floor and I think, this is how it begins.

Hostage of This
Nameless Feeling

At the 5 & Dime you can buy a Fortune-Telling Miracle Fish. A thin transparent red filmy fish shape comes in a plastic envelope made in Taiwan. You take out the fish and place it in the palm of your hand. The fish's movements indicate the state of your love. Moving Head . . . Jealousy. Moving Tail . . . Indifference. Moving Head and Tail . . . True love. Curling Sides . . . Butterflies. Turns Over . . . False. Motionless . . . Fickle. Curls Entirely . . . Gloom and Doom. When you place the fish in your palm it does everything on the list.

I have a feeling about what love is. It saw it in a commercial for a movie when I was a kid. The movie was *The Blue Lagoon*. In the commercial Brooke Shields and some blond guy were on a beach wearing hardly any clothes. The Town Movie Theatre was owned by a Baptist man, which meant no good movies were ever shown. I wanted more than anything to see this movie. I hated the Baptist man for keeping it from me.

In the waiting room of the place where my grandmother got fitted for dentures there was a *People* magazine with *The Blue Lagoon* people on the cover, which I tore off, and once home, hid in my pillowcase. At night I would pull it out and look at it until my eyes adjusted and I could see Brooke Shields and the blond guy. I concentrated on the love in that picture until it was my feeling.

My first "real" kiss. We are at a washateria where smoking is allowed inside. He pulls away. I can't do this, he says. He didn't say it like it was wrong. He just couldn't. Tired from work, two weeks on, two weeks off. Rich men paid Anthony for sex and he snuggled to them like a kitten.

Who couldn't like a girl in a bikini. I like how underneath edges of a bathing suit met skin. The points of
buoyancy between body and bathing suit. I like the flat
stomach and the firm pooch pooled around the navel.
How it sloped downward with small sun-bleached hair
barely visible beneath the navel. I like the shape of their
breasts and how their breasts could hold up the tops. I
like the plane of their chests going into breasts. How
smooth. I like the feet of girls in bikinis. They look
smaller, they look tan. I like how girls in bikinis could
turn from back to stomach, rise and lower. I like how
they were creatures not like me. Chastity Blanco wore a
black bikini and a pearl necklace at the Oakwood
Swimming Pool. The pearl necklace was a trademark.
People said it was a slutty thing to do. Parents should
never name a girl Chastity.

Hey you, she says. Me? You. I think I saw you the other
day, you were walking downtown and you didn't have
on any makeup. Yeah, I say. I was walking. Well why
weren't you wearing any makeup. I forgot, I say. Where.
Where what. Were you walking. Oh I don't know just
walking. That's kind of weird, she says. She sits up then
tells me to follow her. In the girl's bathroom we smoke

a cigarette standing in hot puddles of bleach water. She tells me some guy named Tony told a bunch of guys she did the butterfly with him. What's the butterfly, I ask. I don't know, she says, exhaling. Facing each other I think how she is one wing and I am the other.

A lot of being a kid was walking downtown. It's how I found the abandoned museum. A lot of stuff in the museum had been removed but a lot of stuff was still there. I entered the building through a busted basement window. The basement floor was carpeted in old exploded encyclopedias.

It had been called Town Hall Museum. In it there was a rat-devastated stuffed flying squirrel in a broken glass box next to a mannequin in a rotting hoopskirt. The building was constructed before the Civil War for dancing and performances. There was an open center for waltzing and a raised stage. Above the stage a thick rope drooped from dust weight of red velvet curtain sag. There was a dead dog in the middle of what would have been the dancing floor. When I first broke into the museum the dog was just dead. Over time it became a stain on the floor outlined in gray bristle. The abandoned museum was the greatest place in the world.

All I had to do was be there and look at stuff. Like how I thought church should be plus you could smoke. Smoking a cigarette in the girl's bathroom with Chastity Blanco she tells me about Tony and the butterfly because she saw me walking downtown on a Sunday afternoon without any makeup on, but I do not tell Chastity Blanco about the abandoned museum.

I love girls in bikinis but fucking hate going to the pool. I only go when I have to watch this spoiled kid after which I am given five bucks by the mother who smells like lotion and sleeps in a separate bedroom from her husband.

The next day I buy some spray paint with the five bucks. In the abandoned museum I paint a black arrow on the floor pointing to where the dog had been. I paint the word CHASTITY above the mannequin in the rotting hoopskirt.

• • •

Anthony grabs me by the arm. We run down the long corridor and into the front parlor where no one goes. My sister walks through the house yelling our names. He is pretending to have kidnapped me in order to make love to me and she is pretending to hunt him down so she can kill him. We are in a good hiding place and it takes my sister so long to find us that Anthony pushes me from behind the door. We burst into the unlit corridor. My sister screams, then chases Anthony. They disappear into darkness.

Get Off Your High Horse and
Come to the Party

If you are over twelve you can purchase alcohol. Across the Beau Repose river bridge is The Beer Barn. It is a barn you drive through. When it's your turn you drive into the barn and a girl brings you alcohol. She takes your money to a tired-looking woman sitting on a stool. If the woman can't sell because a cop is around, you drive fifteen minutes down the levee and Jake at Jake's will give you alcohol if you let him look at your breasts while you turn slowly, left right left. After a night of drinking, driving around, and congregating in parking lots, a group ends up at the apartment where my mother and I live. My mother is not there and won't be until her boyfriend is out of drugs. I go to my bedroom to lie down. Hamp Jones follows.

Hamp Jones played football in high school and now plays in college. He is wide with strawberry-colored hair. The headboard of my bed is against the wall and on the other side, rock 'n' roll and beer funneling. Hamp Jones pulls down my jeans and gets on top. Stop I say. It hurt Mandy the first time too he says. I do not know Mandy and he does not stop. After, I walk into the room where the others are. Hamp Jones leaves then everyone leaves. I return to bed and pass out.

I wake naked. I have taken off my clothes during the night but do not remember doing so. I get out of bed, stand in front of a full-length mirror that used to hang in the house of a gay movie star's mother and I look at myself. With the exception of being born, being fucked for the first time, and dying, you generally get another shot at things. Did I say It or did It say it? Something said It. I touch my body and the image in the mirror touches its body.

• • •

Me in a movie dress. Pink/shiny. Red. Always black. Black. Black. Makes you look thin. Slash of lips. The blondest hair. Sculpted into the dress. The woman in every movie comes together in one woman. You can't look at her. Because she is pieces but the pieces are flesh and must connect. Must meld into one movie woman. There are too many movie women that must become this one. It takes too long to figure their best parts, so you swoop. You swoop down and gather the feeling. The feeling of the best part. The feeling is flesh. Soft flesh that melds. The one made, she is best of all. She is in a shiny dress, a red dress, a black dress. Now you must get inside her. You must wear her. But you cannot look at her so you must get there another way. Not the direct way. It's like going to Hawaii [she goes there]. You get on the plane, then you are there. Where were you in the middle? The middle doesn't matter. You must go into it like an airplane does the sky. Like the impossible. You must push yellow ethers through your middle meat. You must get to Hawaii where the others await you for the party.

Make a Joke and I Will Sigh and You Will Laugh and I Will Cry

Decades after *Brown versus the Board of Education* the county decides to desegregate the public schools. There are two public high schools, North and South. The blacks go to North. The whites, South. The new public school combining North and South will be on the South campus and will be called Town. In preparation for the black people a barbed-wire fence is erected and it is announced that there will be security guards. Panic erupts among Southern parents. Children are rapidly withdrawn from what will be Town and placed in Private.

My mother is poor but a benefactor from my grandmother's Catholic church pays for me to attend Private where I cannot make friends because I am weird. One day in history class the girl sitting in front of me turns. Her name is Heather. She asks if I live in the public housing apartments and I tell her yes I live in Kingston Heights. She lives fifteen blocks over on a respectable street of split-level ranchers. That's cool, I say. No it's not, she says, the neighbors think we're freaks. Because you're Chinese, I ask. No, she says, I am not fucking Chinese. Right, I say. My mother is Vietnamese. My father brought her back from the war.

• • •

When Heather is absent one day I take the bus to her neighborhood, and stop by her house to see if she is feeling better. Fucking cramps, she says as she flicks a cigarette. Fuck cramps, I say. She tells me about her ex-boyfriend Jude, what a jerk and I agree. Jude is a total jerk.

Friday night Heather and I go out. We see Jude in the strip mall parking lot where kids hang out. He ignores Heather. We drink more, cursing the bastard. Heather's friend Bitch Michelle drives Heather's mom's station wagon since Heather can't. I lay my head in Heather's lap and say loud that Michelle is a bitch. Heather and I laugh uncontrollably. Bitch Michelle hates us and grips the steering wheel hard.

Later I pass out in my bedroom. When I wake Jude is there, his hands rubbing my breasts, my underwear a cold ball between my feet. My bed is underneath a window and the window is open. I do not know how he knows where I live or which window is my bedroom window or why the window was not locked.

* * *

For Halloween Private School encourages students to dress up. After lunch the whole school shuffles into the gym where there is a haunted house that is not scary, an apple-bobbing event, and a costume contest.

I decide to dress up like a movie star, a real Hollywood girl. At the library I check out a *Reader's Digest* picture book called *Hollywood Damsels and Dames.* I cut out the black-and-white pictures I like best and tape them around the mirror.

My hair is plain and brown but must be Ginger Rogers-platinum in order to make it work. I bleach my hair but it just looks a little lighter and kind of orange. I give myself a beauty mark on my right cheek with eyeliner. I paint my lips red.

I don't have any clothes that can pass as movie star clothes so I borrow a blue dress from my sister's closet. It doesn't fit and looks more like a huge sweater than a dress but at least it doesn't look like a normal dress. Movie stars do not wear normal dresses.

At the Halloween Private School carnival the most popular girl asks me what I am. Before I can answer she says: are you a hooker? No I say. I'm a movie star.

I skip school the next day and bleach my hair until it is luminous of no color.

On my birthday Heather and I split a fifth of vodka and mix it with a peach Nehi. We go to the bar where Anthony works and lives and I tell him today is the day of my birth. It is late and the bar is closed. He asks what I want for my birthday. I tell him what I want is to make love. I go to the kitchen where his mattress is and lie down. He does not follow. Eventually I return to the bar. A short Mexican woman sitting at the bar begins to laugh while Anthony pours her another. The woman is Junkie Carlotta who dresses like Madonna when Madonna was just getting famous.

Heather is given permission to attend an away football game. We tell Heather's parents we are driving with Danielle Doxen and staying with Danielle Doxen's sister who attends Christian College in Big City. I borrow my grandmother's old General Lee since she's now in a nursing home and won't miss it. On the way to Big City we stop at a juke and buy a case of ponies. After a couple Heather says she has something to tell me and she's never told anyone.

She is in love with a man and he loves her. He has moved away but will return. His name is Sean and he's thirty-seven. I swear I will never tell. By the time we arrive at the game to put in an appearance it is over and our team lost.

Some of the bad boys, including Jude, moved to Big City to attend technical college. We spend the night at their apartment. After smoking some pot, Heather and I go to bed. We sleep in Jude's room since we know him best. Jude enters the room and gets in on my side of the bed. He slides a smooth, dry hand between my thighs. Heather gets out of bed and leaves the room. I get out of bed and follow her. Let's leave this shithole, I say. Driving on the highway through gray morning with Heather I feel happier than I have ever felt.

This May Hurt a Little but It's Something You'll Get Used To

Heather and I drive around drinking beer and talking about Sean. I have met Sean, on the night I had a date with this kid Patrick who was graduating. That afternoon a neighborhood girl, Bevy, asked me to go with her to a house where Sean and a bunch of guys lived. He wanted Bevy to bring him a bottle of whiskey, a pack of cigarettes, and something from McDonald's. When we got there he walked into the front room. There wasn't furniture in the room, only a sleeping bag. He had just gotten out of the shower and wasn't wearing a shirt. Who the fuck are you, he said, looking at me. He did not tell Bevy thank you for the whiskey, cigarettes, or McDonald's.

He was thin with shoulder-length blond hair. I had only seen long hair on guys in videos. He wasn't like anyone I actually knew. He poured drinks. I gave Bevy a look but she was going to take one if he was offering. Oh come on, Christ, he said. You'll make your stupid date. I had a drink then had more. What I remember is his wet hair touching his shoulders.

When I finally met up with Patrick I had missed graduation and could barely walk. I told him I couldn't make the ceremony because someone in my family died. When he was a kid, Patrick's brother died in a boating accident and I thought he'd drop it if death was my reason. Later he tried to talk me into giving him head. He had his pants down, his pale ass spread flush to the wet grassy field. By this time I was sober. He put his hand on my head and pushed it down, but I could not put it in my mouth. He told me he was disappointed.

Sean's house is for sale. Empty except for a few contents crammed into the front room: the Kitchen Slash Den. We are standing in the driveway at night. Hey, he says, why don't you take a walk so Heather and I can hang out. On my walk I decide to forget what a jerk he was the day Bevy and I took him whiskey, cigarettes, and McDonald's. When I come back Heather buttons her shirt and we leave.

After Sean moved back to town his mother moved to Pennsylvania because her sister said there was work. Sean lives in the house's Kitchen Slash Den. In it there is a loveseat, two wicker chairs, a coffee table, a small black-and-white television on top of an empty cardboard box, and a cheap stereo. There are some orange juice glasses.

His mother left her bed, but he did not sleep in it. Her room was in the back of the house. It was a haunted house and he felt better living in the part closest to the street. At first we go to the house on weekend nights, then some after school, then every day and as many nights as possible. For me any night is possible.

∙ ∙ ∙

It is immediately established that Sean will take Heather's virginity then they will have sex all the time. I am always with Heather so he says I will do the same with his friend Don who has balls the size of a horse. It will be a big deal, he says, to lose our virginity, to enter the world of doing it. He is so happy when he talks this way I let it slide that I think I may have already entered the world of doing it. I want to be a part of what makes him happy, a part of what is good.

Leading up to the sex he talks to us sexually. He has a theory and guesses the size of our nipples in relation to coins. Heather is a dime and I am a quarter. One night at McDonald's he tells me he can tell by a girl's mouth if she can give head. He thinks I'll be able to. He speaks in sexual pictures that include us. He shows us a picture.

In it a young girl making a sexy face has her shirt off. There are thin red scratches on her face and neck.

Rock Hard, Ride Free

After school drinking Jack Daniels in an orange juice glass is the day I meet Don. Don seemed kind of Native American or something, full of acne scars from when he had been a teenager a long time ago. Now he had gray streaks in his hair. He is there to check me out. He ignores me completely. Sean says, How about some more Jack Daniels to loosen the lips, get it, loosen the lips. No one laughs. Sean plays a song on the stereo about a guy who has a hard-on, then plays a metal tape and he and Don bang their heads.

* * *

The normal crowd is at the house, plus Don. The normal crowd is me, Heather, Sean, his neighbor Stan, Stan's seventeen-year-old stripper girlfriend Stephanie, and a high school dropout who can sing like Axl Rose named Jericho. We are celebrating Stan's forty-fourth birthday. Sean tells me to go to his mother's bedroom and wait. I go. I do not turn on the light. I lay down and feel stupid so I sit up. I wonder how long I am supposed to wait. Don walks into the room and turns on the light. On or off, he asks. Off, I say.

He says, Tell me when you're ready. I'm ready. Already? I say nothing and he proceeds. He positions my ankles on either side of my head. Though this position is unflattering and painful it doesn't hurt the way it is supposed to if you're a virgin so I scratch his chest that there might be pain, even if it's not mine.

After, Sean pours everyone Jack Daniels in the Kitchen Slash Den. He asks how it was. Great I say, trying to appear both enthusiastic and shy. He's got balls the size of a horse don't he, Sean laughs. I look down as if struck dumb by the astonishing size of Don's balls. Don leaves. Not that I have much to compare it to, but I didn't notice that Don had unusually large balls. The next time I see Sean he says, You were no virgin. Yes, I say, I was. He says it again but whispers.

● ● ●

At the apartment, alone. I turn on the stereo. I start to walk through the apartment. I walk faster and faster until I am running. I run through the apartment. In the kitchen, into the den, to the hallway, up the hallway, in the bedrooms, and back again. I go into the place.

Long blond hair, long, thin body, in the shoe shop boots. In the movie girl dress. I go into the place. He is there. I walk into the place. He is there. I turn to say just the thing, what was the thing? Me, illustrious, immaculate, sparkling.

* * *

Christmas break and my sister is home from college. She takes me to Anthony and Junkie Carlotta's annual Christmas party even though it is the first one. Anthony married Junkie Carlotta at the courthouse and now they live in a one-room apartment behind a burned-down gas station. They have a sink, mini-fridge, and hot plate for a kitchen with a toilet behind a sheet in the corner. Between the sink and the mini-fridge a Mexican flag that belonged to Junkie Carlotta's now dead brother is tacked to the wall. There is a ladder that leads to a loft bed.

Claude is home from veterinarian school and is at his cousin's party. At the end of the night I throw up in the front yard. My sister takes me to my mother's then she goes to my grandmother's so she won't have to share a bed with me. Several hours later Claude knocks on my window and I sneak out. We return to Anthony and Junkie Carlotta's. In the loft bed Claude pulls down my jeans. I see thin cuts in the ceiling. In one, a toenail. It belongs to Junkie Carlotta. When I had been at the party the first time she told me she wedges her toes into the ceiling when she and Anthony have sex.

Claude undoes his pants with one hand and covers my mouth with the other. I kick off my shoes and one hits someone below in the face, after which we leave. I do not get the shoe back. We go to Claude's mother's falling-down but still fancy house, famous because once a cannonball came through the roof. It came into what is now Claude's bedroom. This excites me but he tells me to shut up or I will wake his mother and he points to the bed. He puts on Pink Floyd and turns out the light.

He asks if I'm on the pill. I tell him no. He says I am stupid. He punches himself in. Did you let that piece of shit fuck you. Punch. What piece of shit. Punch. I'm not sure who, exactly, he means. Punch. Well just shut the fuck up then. Cocaine and snot smeared across his sweaty face.

· · ·

I will have sex under the condition that it remain a secret and I only pull down my jeans. I do not want Sean to see my breasts since my nipples are bigger than quarters. Let's compromise, he says. Shirt on, jeans off. When he is done he grabs my arms and places them above my head with one hand and pulls my shirt and bra up with the other and he looks. Then releases me, rolls out of bed, lights a cigarette, and walks out of the room. Laying on the bed, my shirt pulled over my face, I can hear laughter and Black Sabbath's *Never Say Die* coming from the Kitchen Slash Den. Another day begins.

• • •

Sean is excited because a girl from Germany gave him some hash she smuggled in by wrapping it in tinfoil and sticking it in her vagina. We smoke it then someone crushes amphetamines and we snort them. I fall backwards into the loveseat. It's O.K., Sean says. I'm sitting between Sean and his neighbor, Stan. You're just feeling it drip down your throat, kind of burning, you just have to let it drip. I wake to slicking. I can hear it. I am in the bed and Stan is having sex with me. My eyes are open but I can't move any part of my body or speak. The bed is soaking. Snap. A polaroid flash.

It can't be done with others. Dead people and God are witnesses. Furniture can be a witness. Eventually, reckon: Dead people, God, and furniture I know you see. So there. But after that, the trapdoor opens into the garden, which leads to the gate. I incised some narrow lines into my palms and between my fingers.

Though discreet, still Heather sees them. You gotta stop that she says. It's better that she knows. It doesn't make me stop, but it's a relief anyway.

***

The group has gone to a creek to drink beer. Heather and I arrive late because on the way we got stuck in the middle of a funeral procession. We are trying to have a picnic but no one knows how. After drinking beer for a couple of hours Sean tells everyone I lied about being a virgin. He sings "I guess that makes you a liar" to the tune of *Gilligan's Island* and the group laughs for the first time all day. Sean cracks open another beer. It's like the picnic starts. That night I wake in the soaking bed. That night and a lot of nights.

* * *

Everyone is passed out in the hallway or in the Kitchen Slash Den. I wake early in the bed. Blue light fills the room. A hand strokes my chest. It is tender, but intentional. No one at the house has ever touched me this way. I open my eyes to see who it is but it is no one. A door closes.

Run to the Hills, Run
for Your Lives

I have missed 80% of the school year and Private School
says I must talk to a special counselor. I like her because
she smokes so I can too. She makes her recommendation
to the state that I attend a Class A reform school. Then I
do not like her. I cry in the parking lot of the Kmart
waiting for the bus. A man in a station wagon pulls up.
Are you O.K., he asks. I am crying hysterically but say, Yes
I am fine. He smiles, rolls up his window, and drives
away. The wagon has a bumper sticker that says I'M A
PROUD SOCCER DAD!

● ● ●

Sitting on the bed in the hot room it is so hot your shirt
sticks to you. The cloth sticks to you. Gentle lifting.
Who lifted it? Hands like willow baskets to soft lips of
mouth. Finger in. Teeth tips locate edge. Bear down
until it almost breaks. Until teeth make skin meet skin.
As much as you want to, do not bite through. From now
on no crying. This scarlet flowing: pinning yourself into
the middle.

At Reform School there is an induction process. The head of the school is Dr. Rails. Before Dr. Rails was a school administrator he was a truck driver. He has retained the body. He closes the door to his office and sits in a squeaky leather chair. His palms rest on a large desk stained to look expensive. Let's you and I have a talk, he says. He takes out a small tape recorder, puts it between us, then pushes record. Tell me about your sex life, he says. I say I don't have one, I'm a teenage girl. He laughs. O.K., he says. Let's start with masturbation. I do not masturbate, I say. Do you think about girls when you touch yourself. I do not think of girls. Do you think of their bodies and how those young bodies glisten.

It is impossible to have sex at Reform School unless you have sex with Dr. Rails. Or almost impossible. Mary O'Brian knows how. Every day from 3:15 until 5:30 there are two forms of mandatory activity. One is some kind of exercise like Walk Around The Track or Jogging In Place. The other has some sort of self-improvement aim like Basket Weaving or Writing Letters To Soldiers. At random intervals you receive a pink slip on your cot telling you to report to a new mandatory activity the following day.

There is one mandatory activity known as Survival. In Survival you run as fast as you can through the dense woods bordering Reform School property. Mississippi woods of kudzu and pine are not intended for this type of physical onslaught. No one ever completes Survival without cuts and bruises.

There are three security monitors but all are too lazy and smart to run through the tangled woods. Two walk to the Stopping Point and wait while one blows the whistle at the Starting Point then goes away. Mary O'Brian does the math and figures there are seven and a half minutes when it is possible to have sex without being observed by a monitor. She tells this kid Danny so he can be ready. They are successful. Word gets around and the boys take turns. Whose turn is decided in advance because seven and a half minutes isn't long. Mary never receives a pink slip telling her she must report to a new activity. Almost every boy at Reform School passes through Survival.

From the Inside Out It All Looks the Same

There are two Family Session weekends a year. If you have been good and achieved Clearance Level v you may return home for a Family Session weekend. They are called Family Sessions because they coincide with holidays. All are drug tested upon return. Girls must go through a reinduction process with Dr. Rails and his tape recorder. I am able to return home for the Christmas Family Session. Everyone is jealous of those that get to go. For a few days those people can be free. They can get drunk, have sex, ride in cars, and go in stores. Those that can leave talk about how they will do all of those things, how they can't wait. When I go home I do those things.

***

I hook up with Heather and her new friends and we go to Heather's manager's apartment. He is the manager of a pizza joint called Pizzaz! It's him and six of his buddies. They hold us upside down while we funnel beer. Later we play strip Uno. When Heather takes off her bra this guy refers to her as The Little Asian Kitty. He would like to know what makes the kitty purr and if she would make purring sounds. After a group attempt we realize we do not know how to make realistic purring sounds.

* * *

In a motel room across from the bed I am in is another bed just like it. In it Stripper Stephanie is on top of some guy then the guy I am with pulls me out of the bed we are in. He pushes me in the bathroom, into the shower, and closes the door. Once inside the bathroom he realizes the light is off and he opens the door, turns it on, then closes the door again. I like the lights on, he says. Do it, he says. Do what, I say. It, he says. I do not know what he means. Do it, he says. Standing in the shower I make a face like I'm a girl in a horror movie.

I do not see Sean over the Christmas Family Session. He left town three weeks before because of trouble. Heather and I are devastated. We do not know what the trouble was.

On my last night home we drive around drinking beer. What are you going to do, I ask. She looks straight ahead and says that once she's done with high school, they'll move to Vietnam and start an organic farm. Then they'll be together forever.

Darling, Do You Wear the Mask

Square Dancing is a mandatory activity. It is taught by Miss Lafitte, one of the Solitary Confinement monitors. It happens in an oblong empty room. Everyone in Square Dancing is assigned a partner.

When assignments were going out I hoped to Jesus not to be paired with Rorrie. I was paired with Rorrie. Rorrie had a sweating problem. Thick sweet oil coated his black hair and made his palms slippery. Rorrie was the kid who ran everywhere.

They tried to control this through medication and punishment, but it didn't work. Rorrie ran everywhere because in grade school he got a tardy and his father made him run barefoot over a broken whiskey bottle so he would learn the meaning of run. Rorrie also had a condition that made his breathing sound funny. Being Rorrie's partner meant we were the fastest square dancers in Square Dancing though Rorrie couldn't really square dance, he could only run.

Miss Lafitte wore a purple leotard over light purple tights. She had bad posture and her flabby belly hung from her rib cage. She would stand on a wooden box next to the record player and call out the moves.

In Square Knot four sets of couples link arms and move squarishly in a circle. First the circle goes clockwise. Then counterclockwise. After the couple originally in the twelve o'clock position returns to the twelve o'clock position, all couples take four galloping steps backwards, skip around one another, then take four galloping steps forward. After which you change partners with the couple directly in front of you. Kandy was directly in front of me. She gave me a look that expressed how awful everything was. After that I hoped Kandy was always directly in front of me. She often was.

Every time I dossie-doed away from Kandy I would try and see her face. It was serious like she was concentrating. The fat around her jaws quivered because she stomped her feet so hard.

· · ·

Miss Lafitte makes everyone stop because the record player needle is skipping. Kandy is my partner and we are standing shoulder to shoulder, my right hand is holding Kandy's left and my left hand is holding her right. I let my right hand slip so that my thumb lands on her wrist. I do not look at Kandy and she does not move her hand away. I move my thumb back and forth across Kandy's wrist.

* * *

Kandy and I get to know each other.

Can you imagine Miss Lafitte giving a blow job. No. It was impossible to imagine. She probably gave blow jobs all the time when she was young and now she's too slutty to get a real husband. Probably. We longed for cigarettes. What I wouldn't do for a motherfucking cigarette.

What do you want to be when you grow up.
Me: a cosmetologist. Kandy: a mechanic.

She once puked a Big Mac on this guy she was doing it with because she was so drunk. It was the funniest thing I'd ever heard.

The nubby scar on Kandy's wrist felt like splatter that had solidified. There are two ways to slit your wrists, Kandy said. The first way is to slice horizontals and try to sever the veins, which is how most people do it. The second way is the no-fucking-around way. You take the razor but instead of just cutting a horizontal you slice in and rake up. That's the way I did it, she said.

Kandy told me how her father died. These guys came in the house and took him into the other room and tied him up. They poured gas on him, lit a match, and he burned. A neighbor called the fire department before Kandy burned up in the playpen. They never got the guys who did it. She said her father probably had a gambling debt he couldn't pay. Shit, I said, Jesus Mary and Joseph. Well, she said, he was always in some kind of trouble.

* * *

In October two girls escape from Reform School. The girls are either idiots or Yankees. One drowns in the Mississippi River while trying to swim to Louisiana.

The girl who lived returned to Reform School and tried to kill herself a week later by drinking a bottle of Sun-In hair lightener she had hidden in her mattress. After that they took her to a mental hospital.

The day they take the girl away I wake during the night. Kandy's thick hands over my mouth. My mouth is open and I can taste Kandy's fingers. She presses down hard to tell me to shut up then gets under the covers and spoons in behind me. *I've never told anyone something.* Well you can tell me.

Our arms are linked and we are moving in a circle. A chorus optimistically "woo-hoos!" Every time Kandy and I meet in the line we swing each other as hard as we can. Around we go. When the record finishes Miss Lafitte raises her arms triumphantly, says, Give hand and bow. Traverse to partner.

Crazy but That's How It Goes

After a year I am released from Reform School on probation. The benefactor kicks down for Private School but I must write a letter saying Thank You and that I am now an improved person. The benefactor writes back in the scratchy handwriting of old people that I should trust in God and avoid gaining excess weight. I like the scratchy handwriting and put the letter in a shoebox along with a picture of my mother dressed up like a little bride while receiving her first communion.

We are taping black-and-white magazine pictures of Andy Warhol to the walls of the bedroom Heather shares with three sisters, all unfortunately under the age of six, when the phone rings. It's Sean.

Heather clutches the phone, Where are you. With people, he says, far away. As far as California. As far as that. Yeah but like where. Listen, he says, I've got this friend. He's in a band that's about to be big time. I'm their lead singer, anyway he saw your picture and thinks you're hot. Shut the fuck up, Sean. Oooh someone's in a bad mood. Fucking shut up I Miss You. He doesn't shut the fuck up and Heather throws the phone on the bed. I pick it up. So do you want to talk to him. Who, I say. My friend. Talk about what. You know. Sexy things. No I do not, I want to talk to you. But then he vanished.

* * *

Jude knocks on the door of my mother's apartment. After technical school he moved back, got work on a construction crew, and lived in a trailer behind his sister's house. He comes over again the next night. We begin to hang out even though it's weird because he used to be with Heather. I do not ask about the night I woke and he was in my bed rubbing my breasts into blisters. Eventually, he becomes my boyfriend.

For my birthday Jude rents a room at the Ekono Inn for three hours so I can demonstrate what I've learned in the *Newly Revised Joy of Sex* book he bought for me at the mall. The book isn't helpful but in the newly revised version there are photographs of people having sex instead of hippy drawings.

When we went into the motel room he made me turn on the light. A small felt bag was taped to the switch. Inside it there was a tacky necklace in the shape of a horseshoe. If you're good, he said, matching ring for Christmas.

． ． ．

My English teacher takes me out of the regular class and puts me in the advanced one. In the advanced class all you do is read books and it is much better than the other stupid class. The first book we read is about a woman living in old-timey days who is married to a boring guy so she has an affair with a guy who's younger and clever in all the ways her boring husband isn't. There aren't any sex scenes, it's all implied.

Sleeping with the younger guy makes the woman feel great and also shows her how shitty her life really is. She does something unheard of and gets her own place down the street from the house her husband owns. Everyone thinks she's nuts. Even though she has her own place and it's decorated really nice with a great chandelier she realizes things won't work out in a favorable way so she kills herself by swimming, something she was never good at, by letting herself be taken to sea.

For my response essay I begin with the sentence: There are worse things than enduring sadness. The teacher reads it out loud. I shoot this girl Bitch Lisa a look like: fuck you, I'm deep.

I admire that the woman had the guts to get her own place. I think about her death. It is romantic and sad. But at least she got to have her own place.

* * *

I get a strep infection that spreads to my kidneys and I must be hospitalized. In the hospital I have a miscarriage. My mother and sister find me in the bathroom sitting in a pool of blood. It is the brightest blood any of us had ever seen. Later, a nurse talks to me about getting pregnant. You don't want that she says. Believe me, she says. And don't think I don't know what you're doing. She says so directly, with black sparkling eyes. The next morning a doctor comes in with a group of medical students I can't look at in case one of them is Claude even though Claude is a veterinarian student somewhere else. The doctor puts on a pair of latex gloves and tells me to open my legs. I open my legs and he puts his hand inside then pulls it out. He turns to face the students raising his slick gloved hand like he is saying How and they are Indians. The students write something on clipboards then leave. Jude comes to visit and says I was never really pregnant. Are you sure? I ask. Yes, he says. Really, I say, because I think I lost your child, and I think it was a boy. You weren't pregnant, he says. But I can tell it really bothered him. So I say it again.

* * *

Anthony dies and I keep thinking the first person who kissed me for real is dead. The circumstances of his death are ambiguous. He definitely died in the empty lot behind a Mexican restaurant. He definitely was beaten. But by whom and for what reason.

Possible reasons suggested at a bar after the funeral: 1) Anthony was having an affair with Junkie Carlotta's dead brother's wife, and the dead brother's wife's boyfriend murdered Anthony. 2) He met a bad man in the park. After all, the park bordered the Mexican restaurant, and Anthony was a rent boy. 3) Anthony was a petty thief and was caught and killed [though technically that Anthony was a petty thief is a rumor, it is still allowed]. 4) Junkie Carlotta beat him to death. At the bar no one says number 4 out loud to the group, which includes Junkie Carlotta. Everyone believes number 4.

Stripper Stephanie who was sleeping with Anthony behind Junkie Carlotta's back is the most angry about it. She grips her beer until her knuckles go white. The rest of us understand it was an accident.

Anthony's casket was middle range. More than a pine box but no platinum vault. At the two-month marker I imagine his face greening into its cavities. At three, his fingers beginning to twist. At four, a fine chalk of dried organs needled with brittle ends of hair. Thereafter, stains on mauve satin. When I was a kid I wrote love letters to Anthony and hid them from my sister in the Bible, a place I knew she would never look. Just in case I gave him the secret code name: Lance. There were times I would wake at dawn, take the Bible outside, and sit on the other side of the camellia bush. I'd smoke cigarettes, drink Tang, touch the cover of the Bible in a pious way, and cry because I loved Anthony so much.

Master, Master Where's the Dreams I've Been After

After graduation I started to break it off with Jude. I was going to college in Big City. It didn't seem likely I would but this college let me write an essay explaining why I should get to come even though my grades were atrocious. Jude did not want me to go to college, he wanted me to marry him. We would live in the trailer behind his sister's house and have a baby. He wanted to remake the lost baby. He said it was his right.

When I started to break it off, Jude got weird. Leaving the apartment there was Jude crouched in the bushes, fingers in mouth, laughing. Eventually Jude got violent. When he did it was toward his retarded brother, Daryl. He broke a bottle, picked up one of its shards, pointed it at Daryl saying, Don't tell me who I can or can't play with.

Because we were still in contact through the break-up process he called and told me he had done this. I didn't ask why but remembered the story Jude told me in which his uncle beat his seven-year-old ass for being friends with a black kid. When Jude told me this story it was to tell me sometimes in life we have to do things we don't want to but we should because they are right. It was right not to play with the black kid but he would have kept doing it had his uncle not beat his ass. He told me this story after he told me I couldn't smoke dope with anyone but him because girls would just sleep with anyone if they smoked dope.

One night Jude called and told me to look out the window. No, I said. Just look out, he said. I opened the curtains but didn't see anything. I see you, he said. I'm what they call a Watcher. What's that, I asked. Can't tell you, he said, It's high up. Really fucking high up. Like how high, I said. Like other beings, he said. Looking out of the window I saw nothing and I gave it the finger.

· · ·

The summer before college Stripper Stephanie, Heather, and I go to Daytona Beach to experience the Floridian partying we have heard so much about. Heather pays my way using money she saved from Pizzaz! and she uses saved-up allowance money to pay for everything else. We take enough alcohol to kill us.

In Daytona we have a room with a kitchenette at the Aloha Chalet Motel. Everything in the Aloha Chalet is chained to the floor or wall. A guy with a foul disposition works the lobby. As soon as we arrive it starts to rain. No matter how much we drink we cannot get drunk. The stretch of beach in front of the Aloha Chalet is ugly. You can rent pornos in the lobby but only one at a time. It means getting the lobby guy to get the movie from inside a glass case then you have to tell him what room you are in so he can put it on your bill. For an additional price you can rent one of the crappy duct-taped VCRs. We rent a VCR and every movie. They are locally produced. In them women have sex in wood-paneled rooms with guys who have hairy chests and beer guts.

· · ·

Our second night in Daytona we decide to go to Gators. It is Ladies Night at Gators, which means male dancers. The club is at maximum capacity with sweaty women drinking Blue Balls, the official alcoholic beverage of Gators.

You can't really see the dancers because there are so many women and they are all going crazy standing on chairs, railings, and tables. Eventually the dancers leave the stage and begin working the crowd. Even though you can't see the dancers you can tell they are in the crowd because women form in flocks throughout the room making tight smoky circles, screaming.

One of the dancers comes to where we are standing. A middle-aged woman with a bleached-out frizzy perm has a cigarette and Blue Balls in one hand, a buck in the other. The dancer is a short Italian-looking guy who is shiny and smells like coconuts. He is only wearing a g-string but you can't see the g-string because of all the dollar bills. You know the g-string is there because of the tutu of bills. Something has to be holding the bills.

The dancer is close to the woman, grinding his hips. I pluck one of the bills from the tutu. It is a knee-jerk reaction like taking a piece of candy from a candy dish even if you aren't going to eat it. The dancer feels it, turns to face me, and snatches the dollar from my hand. What the fuck do you fuck think you're doing you fuck. I try and explain it was an accident but the mood is shattered for the women and they become angry.

After we are escorted out of Gators we return to the Aloha Chalet. The phone rings. It's Jude. He wrangled the motel number from Stripper Stephanie's new gay boyfriend by buying him shots of tequila at a Louisiana disco across the state line. He'd been threatening his brother again.

Look, I say, it's over. Oh no it's not, he says. It's not over until the fat lady screams. Don't you mean sings, I ask. No, he chuckles, I don't. I scream, then hang up.

The Only Good Indians
Are Tame

After the Aloha Chalet I must go to Big City College Orientation Weekend. The weekend is designed to acclimate incoming students to collegiate life. It happens during summer so only some of the students are on campus. You are assigned a gender appropriate buddy. My buddy is Allisa. She is the kind of girl that is called cute. Allisa is a Delta Phi Delta. This is how it works, Allisa says. There's Delta Phi Delta, Chi Delta, Kappa Omega, and Phi Kappa. Every girl is something. The Delta Phi Deltas and Chi Deltas are party girls. Even though they party they still have good reputations. A Delta Phi Delta girl has made the cover of the Lambda Alpha Fraternity fundraiser calendar six years running. The Chi Deltas party with the guys from Pi Kappa Alpha and the Delta Phi Deltas party with the Lambdas. The Kappa Omegas are all virgins with red hair but not really because they do it with their Alpha Kappa Alpha boyfriends but only once they know for sure they'll marry them. You don't want to go Phi Kappa. That's where the weird girls end up that no one else wants. She asks me if I want to be in a sorority. I tell her I don't think so.

After the first day of campus tours, placement tests, and Meeting Faculty and Staff, Allisa takes me to a party where I meet Jack. At the party a group of people sit around passing a joint. They are talking about Camus and his book, *The Stranger*. Jack says it's the greatest book ever. The next day I get *The Stranger* and read it when I'm supposed to be attending Meeting Campus Services. I think it's O.K. but don't get the big deal. Jack is fixated on a melancholic girl named Emily spelled French style, Emileè. Allisa says a lot of guys are in love with her. I will learn later Emileè has to return to Pasadena for a family emergency and never returns, thank Jesus.

The next night I see Jack at another party. The party moves to the girl's dormitory because someone there has a bong or beer or a movie about Jim Morrison even though boys aren't allowed after six and it is after six. Once there Allisa pukes in the stairwell after telling this kid Scott that in order to bond with his yin energy he needs to fuck a guy. She tells him how, before she transferred, back at Dartmouth they had orgies and that it was a good thing. After she pukes Scott carries her upstairs and I help him put her in her bed. I do not know what yin energy is and am surprised Allisa went to orgies. I say to Scott she doesn't look like the orgy type so I guess you never know. Scott looks at Allisa's now tranquil face and says in a thoughtful way that they were probably tame, after all they were at Dartmouth and how fucked up could a Dartmouth orgy be. Allisa looks like an angel lying there and I feel compassion for her. That she tried to have an orgy, even if it was at a place called Dartmouth.

The party continues in this girl Stacy's room. Jack and I end up talking and he places his hand in mine. I am in love. Not like the other times and I never really loved Jude. Jack isn't like any guy I know.

Later, we end up in the bathroom. We are kicked out of the dorm when the R.A. finds us in the shower not showering but half naked making out. The next morning in his bed he reaches over me, grabs a pack of cigarettes, lights two, and puts one in my mouth. No one has ever done anything like that to me before. It's the kind of thing that happens to girls in movies. But this is no movie. It's my real life. Jack looks really beautiful, and I think, This is how it begins.

I have an aunt in New Orleans so I go there to wait out the rest of summer before College. I read a book about Geronimo and every morning walk down Magazine Street where I buy a fifty-cent coffee and smoke cigarettes.

Geronimo said Indian warriors should run in a single-file line so the enemy wouldn't know how many of them there were if he found their tracks. I thought that was pretty good.

—— II ——

Religious Studies

Term I

Term II

Term I

My roommate is Susan who has severe arthritis in her knees and must walk with a cane. One day I return from class and Susan has moved out. On mint green stationery she wrote that she needed to move to a room on the ground level [arthritis, etc]. She hopes I have a great semester! May God bless me. Then I have my own room. Next door to me lives my College Orientation Weekend buddy, Allisa.

Do you want to go to a poetry reading, Allisa says. O.K., I say. Do you want to drink some Hawaiian Punch and rum first. O.K., I say. She loves a kid named Mac. They slept together once. I tell her about Jack, how we hooked up over orientation weekend. Were you the girl doing it in the shower, she says. Yeah, I say. I heard about that, she says. We weren't really doing it, I say, I mean we did it, but not in the shower. Have you ever actually done it in the shower, she asks. Not exactly, I say. I did it in the shower once, she says. With Mac, I ask. No, she says, with Chad and Thad. Were they twins, I ask. No, she says, that would have been weird.

* * *

A bunch of people decide to take LSD. Allisa and I have never taken it. We chew the little white square, grinding it with our teeth, then swallow it. An hour later while watching *Fantasia* I start to feel something achy crawl up my spine, then I notice purple smoke coming out of the TV. Wow, I say. Yeah, Allisa says, Groovy.

We take bong hits then everyone takes a walk. On the walk we see a scary clown-trickster made visible because of our connection with the universe. Jack and I take turns being born out of a large water drainage pipe that runs under College View Drive. He crosses the street, enters the tunnel. On the other side of the street I crouch and look into the tunnel. It is dark and we can't see each other until the very end when he emerges, falls into my arms, and is born. Then it's my turn.

On the soccer field Allisa pulls out a glow stick and ties it to a shoelace. It's a space lasso, she says, and begins swinging it in a vertical circle between us, which gener- ates a golden bubble we are inside of. Once the lasso really gets going it creates an invisible past life mirror between us that allows us to see one another's incarnations in rapid succession.

Later Jack and I go to his place. We watch the sun rise through his bedroom window. I think, hold this. No matter what happens later.

··· ·

I offer flowers. I sow flower seeds. I plant
flowers. I assemble flowers. I pick flowers. I
pick different flowers. I remove flowers. I seek
flowers. I offer flowers. I arrange flowers. I
thread a flower. I string flowers. I make flowers.
I form them to be extending, uneven, rounded,
round bouquets of flowers. I make a flower
necklace, a flower garland, a paper of flowers, a
bouquet, a flower shield, hand flowers. I thread
them. I string them. I provide them with grass.
I provide them with leaves. I make a pendant of
them. I smell something. I smell them. I cause
one to smell something. I cause him to smell. I
offer flowers to one. I offer him flowers. I provide him with flowers. I provide one with flowers. I provide one with a flower necklace. I
provide him with a flower necklace. I place a
garland on one. I provide him with a garland. I
clothe one in flowers. I cover him in flowers. I
love him with flowers.

This is an actual song, Teacher says.

Teacher tells us to take out a piece of paper and write down what we think it means. After a few minutes he tells us to stop writing. He points to me: What kind of song do you think this is? A love song, I say. Hmmm, he says.

I love the song more than any song, ever. It's like I wrote it or was just about to. It annoys me that it is already written. This is the song about my love for Jack.

A kind of love song, Teacher says. The kind sung to Aztec gods before performing human sacrifice.

The phone is disconnected so I send my mom a postcard to tell her I'm coming home for Break. When my ride drops me off it is afternoon. As I walk toward the building I cannot tell what the story is. There is always this walk of not knowing. It ends when my hand is on the doorknob, turning it, the door making its pop, the air in the apartment yielding onto my face.

It smells like ashtrays and the curtains are drawn. In the kitchen there is a grocery bag on the counter. It looks like the only things purchased were potato chips and a chicken breast. I close my eyes and feel the hum of the apartment: it has been at least two days since she was here.

I take the bus to Heather's. Heather goes to an expensive out-of-state college and I haven't seen her since we both shipped out. Heather's not home, says Heather's mom who seems tired standing at the door wearing a red terry cloth muumuu holding a martini glass even though it's only three o'clock. Through the open door I can see Heather's baby sister. She is on the floor playing with a pair of chopsticks.

She hasn't called me back since the first week of school, I say. Heather is busy studying the pre-medicine, she says How you do at school? she asks. Great, I say. Studying hard? Yep, I say. Well that's nice. Please tell Heather to call me, I say. If I talk to Heather, she says, I tell her.

My mom comes home late. I ignore her. She makes something gross to eat, but falls asleep sitting up before ever taking a bite. She wakes the next afternoon. After a while she comes in my room and sits on the end of my bed. I am reading. I put my book down and light a cigarette. Well kiddo, she says, we try and sometimes we fail. Yeah, I say. It means she's doing coke again. It means we're back on the Death Watch. I slip my hand in her hand. She squeezes my hand hard.

• • •

Jack and I cruise dark streets of the last good neighborhood bordering campus looking for deep shadows. We end up in the empty parking lot of the First Baptist Church under an oak tree. At least it is dark and inspires a sense of privacy, even if fake. Jack and I make out while a security guard watches in the distance. By the time we notice him my bra is off and I am laughing so hard I cry.

* * *

Jack's friend Pete calls an hour before the show. Wear something weird, he says. What the fuck ever, Allisa says. Yeah what the fuck ever, I say. That's weird, she says. Yeah, I say. I mean, what the fuck. As we put the finishing touches on our outfits we grasp to somehow make them weirder. By the time we get to Jack's we're a six pack each into the night. On the way to the show Jack is distant. He hasn't wanted to go to the First Baptist Church all week and I don't know why. He avoids me after lunch when everyone is sitting around smoking cigarettes.

By the time the band has finished playing I am drunk. I pronounce, loudly, esoteric things in Jack's direction. Enter Harvesters of Sorrow! I say.

I wake depressed. I can't get out of bed. Allisa comes to check on me when she doesn't see me at lunch. She places her hand on my back. Listen, she says, so you got a little Stevie Nicks last night.

I pull myself out of bed midafternoon and call Jack to see if we can talk. When I ask I use my rubbed-raw-can't-we-just-be-humans voice. It's over, he says. Why? I say. It just is, he says. I start to cry. Do you think there is a chance for us in the future? I ask. No, he says, I don't. I carefully place the phone back on the receiver.

* * *

It's like I live that song, I say. Allisa shoots this girl Debbie a look that implies eye roll. They are tired of hearing me talk about Jack and the Flower Song.

We sit around and drink until it's time to go out. At the bar I look for Jack and place myself in proximity until he leaves the scene, which is always too soon. Then I stop seeing him out at all. I don't know where he goes or what he does.

I begin to hang out with Shelly who is in love with Robert who does not love her back. Shelly is a born-again Christian during a confused time, which means she can hang out with me, pine for Robert, and drink malt liquor night after night. Eventually Shelly gets saved again, then it's just me.

Sitting in the darkness, hands around the glass neck of a beer, my mouth makes the shape of words, but no sound comes out. I am imagining. I am wearing a black dress and am beautiful. Jack, Sean, Don, and Claude are there. I am always turning to face them. Always saying just the thing.

One night I come to. I am not asleep, but it is as if I awake. The stereo is on, but tuned between stations so there is loud static. I am standing in front of the mirror. I am moving from foot to foot, kind of swaying. It scares me.

Term II

A famous lady writer comes to College and reads from her new book. It is a big event and tickets are sold to the public. In recalling her early writing days and at the same time summing up his introduction, a man says, "the writer who was so good she had to leave the South." Applause. He is alluding to a story he told as a way of beginning his introduction: early on at Mississippi University her talent was recognized and she was urged to head North where it could receive proper cultivation.

It made me mad. It was like if you had any talent you had to leave. What if you couldn't leave? Why couldn't you be talented where you were. Or what if no one notices your talent, then I guess you're really screwed. Like what if talent only counted when it was noticed by an outside party who knew how to get North.

I realize I feel talented. But in what way? I can't afford to wait for recognition, the opportunity to properly cultivate myself, or even information regarding what, in particular, my talent might be. To hell with waiting, so I get up and leave.

Jamie and Madison were in the same fraternity. They secretly disliked one another and avoided each other so I didn't think it was a big deal to date them at the same time and how can you declare a favorite until you've tried both. Still, it did not go over well, at which point they began competing with each other. Which made the sex better.

One kiss, he said. Boom, pants down. There was no lingering. Jamie said sex should be dirty, which is why he was not afraid of blood or anything. Madison was slower but all over the place. He was into place. They were different kinds of sex and I liked experiencing the alternating forms consistently. Not in a selfish way, but in a what my Intro to Liberal Studies teacher would call a Human Interest way. Then Jamie and Madison got drunk and fought. After they were bloody and crying they fell into each other's arms. Man, what's become of us, dude, we're brothers.

Word of this spread, which turned into a moral story about girls thinking they could dissolve fraternal bonds, which of course is impossible. Jamie and Madison kept coming to my room on alternating nights, each keeping it a secret from the other. Then Jamie and Madison got drunk and fought. They skipped the crying and bloody bit and the situation resolved in what my Intro to Psychology teacher would call Connected Knowing, a form of bonding achieved, in this instance, through laughter: at least they were getting laid. Which made the sex terrible. Which made it mean.

I tell Helene about Jamie and Madison. Helene has short black hair, pale skin, and delicate, pointy features. Her narrow body is draped across my floor, open books around her, her head propped with one hand, smoking a hand-rolled cigarette with the other. We are partners for Women & Contemporary Issues and have been working in my dorm room on our presentation about the history of abortion.

You were doing what men do all the time, she says. If you were a man it would be acceptable but because you're a woman you're a slut. Typical, she says. It's almost impossible for a woman to experience pleasure in our culture, she says. We decide to take a wine break and talk about women, culture, and pleasure. Helene says there's a lot more to pleasure than most women know.

＊　＊　＊

I decide I will major in Theater. After I try out for a play
and don't get a part, I become an English major. In the
English Department all anyone wants to talk about is the
author, never the interesting stuff in the books. I declare
myself a Religion major after attending a lecture given by
Dr. Kyser. Dr. Kyser has a mysterious husband from Haiti
no one has ever seen. They were married while she did
her Religious Studies PhD research in his village. In the
lecture she said she once saw a Shaman shit an egg.

* * *

This is my favorite part of the day. Classes are over. I do not have to be anywhere. I sit on my bed. My bed is beneath a big window, which I open. I light a candle, incense, and a cigarette. I take pinch hits, blowing the pot smoke into a pillow, then quickly take drags off my cigarette to produce more cigarette smoke to help mask the pot smell. After I'm high, I light another cigarette to enjoy since the one I just put out was a work cigarette.

I don't think about Jack so much anymore. Sometimes I think about my mom. She is like a pencil drawing that is slowly being erased. I imagine the picture as it once must have been. In it there is a waterfall, a unicorn, flowers, and soft grass.

What I dread is dinner. Having to go to the cafeteria, interact. When night comes I go to Helene's. When we are studying, in bed, or drinking wine and talking, I feel normal. When I'm alone it's different. But I'd rather be alone.

* * *

Sex with Helene is good or bad. When sex is good sometimes it is encouraged by afternoon light streaming through Helene's attic apartment window or sometimes forethought on the part of Helene. When it is bad it is because Helene is fussy. On these occasions I do everything I know her to like, but my efforts are never quite right and she eventually collapses in frustration after which she is distant and bitchy.

The last time I have sex with Helene she introduces a sex toy. Helene in forethought mode. After, Helene gets out of bed, angry. She lights a cigarette and props her naked body against the dresser. You know, she says, one of the things about women being together is they can leave that male bullshit behind, it really makes me tense when you appropriate patriarchal desire paradigms and make me suffer through them. Oh, I say, I didn't know I was doing that. Oh my god, she says, like hello.

I don't know, she says, maybe Julia's right. Who the hell is Julia, I ask. Julia says you're insecure and as a result can't stand authentic vulnerability. Well maybe you should fuck Julia, I say. Helene looks at me, drops her cigarette in a half empty coke bottle. It sizzles. I am fucking Julia, she says.

The truth is that I really don't like Helene as a person and this news is a relief. Nonetheless I cry like a blabbering idiot. Is there something wrong with me, I blabberask. Helene gets a sad look on her face then the sad look vanishes. You don't make me want to grow, she says.

I don't say anything, just stare into nothing until I realize I'm actually staring at a purple dildo optimistically saluting me from a tangle of sheets.

* * *

One day in Religion seminar we have a special guest. The guest is a chubby redheaded guy from Germany who now teaches Theology at a Scottish University that has joined forces with our school to create an international degree exchange program. I decide I will participate in this program. The next day I make an appointment with my advisor and begin the necessary paperwork. I take placement tests and score exceptionally high. I qualify for a scholarship.

Before leaving for Scotland, I read books, take classes, and work at a dentist's office to save some money. I write my sister a letter to tell her the news, then go home to tell my mom, but she's not around. I wait three days, then just leave a note.

I learned some things. The ancient Greek woman unfurled a red carpet in such a way it seemed to come from her vagina. Her man stepped on it—was pulled toward his bloody fate. Comedies are really tragedies. If you want a tragedy, read a comedy. There was a time on this planet when dragonflies had twenty-eight-inch wingspans. In cafeterias people sit in patterns that mirror actual social hierarchies. Water is the most important substance. Everything would die without it. Realizing the Age of Reason, he tried to get to something original. This move was an unconscious yet accurate appropriation of ancient Taoist practices. There had never been any female philosophers, strangely. Suicide was a debatable subject. Life, whose choice is it? White straight affluent culture is the culture represented. "Thou knowest, said Hester . . . though knowest that I was frank with thee." Walking the red carpet means hell to pay, yet how clever of the woman. To inhabit the metaphor with such bodily ferocity.

III

The Slaughterhouses of Glasgow

Sojourning in a Foreign Land
Threshed with Guts

Here, This Speck and This Speck
You Missed

And Suddenly I Thought:
This Is What It Means to Make a
Movie in Sweden

Aboard, My Love! The Sun Is a
Profound Gamble: Another Day
and Still Another

There Is a Host in Ghost

Sojourning in a 𝔍oreign Land
𝔗hreshed with Guts

After tuition is paid to the Scottish University most of the scholarship money is gone. When I investigate the possibility of getting more I am told to eat bread with cheese and drink wine, it is an overseas adventure.

• • •

Once, the tenement had been a grand house. Thick plaster molding like wedding cake icing lined the ceilings. A carved banister accompanied the interior's wide steps. Now it was a shithole falling into the Kelvin River.

The building had three floors and a basement. On the top floor University dropouts lived off the dole and ecstasy. On the second floor there were two rooms. Five Ukrainian guys shared one and I had the other. On the first floor, the drunk Mochè's room, and in the basement, Ken's office. Ken owned the place. He lived in the office but still called it the office. He wore a gray sweatsuit or some variation of a gray sweatsuit and had three pairs of underwear. He would wash the underwear in the bathroom sink then hang them on the garden fence to dry. He had Speedo-style underwear, colored and shiny. If all three pair were on the fence I knew Ken was not wearing underwear.

The entire building was carpeted in remnants taken from street corners where trash of other torn-down tenements awaited pickup. In places where the floor was rotting there were layers of remnant scraps. You knew where the rotting places were because the carpet would sog in cushioned depressions. Decades of bad paint jobs meant every room was a bunch of peeling and different colors. In my room I counted eleven colors including the color of all colors black.

The building had one bathroom with a shower and toilet. Like everything in the building, if you wanted electricity you had to pay for it as you used it. Hot water for the shower, ten pence a minute. The bathroom was between my room and the five Ukrainian guys'. Its vent emptied into my room so it smelled like shit for hours at a time. I complained to Ken. That's fucking outrageous, he said, fucking shocking.

Outside was a broken sign propped against the entrance railing. It had a dancing red bell pepper on it. The dancing red bell pepper was smiling, wearing black shoes on its bell pepper feet, and had musical notes around its head. It was exclaiming in cartoon letters: Red Pepper Station! Red Pepper Station was the name of the building and Ken's record label.

Ken had projects. He could never talk about them because deals were at stake. Whenever the projects came up he pointed to a framed photo hanging in the office. In the picture Ken stands next to a man he says is Michael Jackson's father.

Sometimes Ken worked as Rod Stewart. It wasn't his idea but it exhausted him to resist, what can you do people are demanding, fucking shocking. I do not think he looks like Rod Stewart but his shiny underwear does remind me of Rod Stewart. It depresses me to think of thick-ankled Scottish women gathered in musty bingo halls watching him lip sync "If You Want My Body" and "Forever Young."

* * *

I meet Ian after my first month at University. Not at one of the University pubs. I do not like University pubs. Urban slick, they make me nervous.

Ruth introduces me to the Shipyard Pub. Ruth was once a Lutheran minister's wife. Now she is Ken's "associate" who sometimes works in Ken's "office." The way her hips sink into chairs I know she had grace before it got used up. The Lutheran got everything in the divorce. She has a picture of three girls in her wallet. In it the girls wear the same dress though they are different ages. It is an old picture.

I like Ruth better than the people at University even though she's fucked up. At first I feel bad then I think how everyone is some kind of fucked up and unlike people I know at University Ruth is nice by which I mean she doesn't judge. The people I meet through the International Exchange Program in The Postmodern Seminar for the Study of Interpretive Uses judge everything.

* * *

I am to find community in my host University's program: a supportive community of colleagues invested at the round table of learning where we gather to explore our cross-cultural concerns in a celebratory discourse of questioning.

My college credits and high scores on the British placement tests puts me at a year and a half to two years before graduating with a Religion degree from Scottish University. Scottish University's Religion department is progressive. Its seminar is called The Postmodern Seminar for the Study of Interpretive Uses. Students must attend the seminar where they participate in co-creating postmodern happenings in honor of Jacques Derrida while also researching and writing a thesis.

* * *

Ian joins Ruth and me at the pub though he isn't drinking. A Scottish guy in a pub not drinking is weird. I ask
him what's wrong with him. He says he can't, when he
does he gets smashed then uses all his methadone instead
of rationing it like he's supposed to. When he says so he
looks kind of spiritual, like a hermit in the desert where
there is fake water everywhere but none to drink.

Once Ruth and I are drunk Ian says little things and we
laugh. Not because he's funny but he doesn't talk much
so it feels like a treat or something so we laugh. A thick
scar runs from the top of his right temple to the right
corner of his mouth. A knife made the scar. That he
hardly talks coupled with a mysterious knife scar is a sex
appeal plus. We go to the pub every night. Every night
Ian sits near me. In this way I begin to love him. Because
he communicates through nearness and the patient
suffering of it.

One night Ruth is wasted and Ian helps me get her back to
Red Pepper Station. After Ken takes Ruth to the office I
lead Ian upstairs. In the terrible room I run my fingers
across the scar then I undress him. He has a man's body.
On his arms, shitty prison tattoos, under the tattoos, blue

veins webbing muscle. After I have pleasure, he has plea-sure. Then he gets out of bed, goes to the bathroom, takes a cold shower, comes back to bed, and sleeps. He does not use his mouth. He does not hold. He is not sentimental. It happens again then again. After I have pleasure, he has pleasure. He showers. He moves in. We live near, silent.

Like every Glasgow ex-con Ian works at the fruit and veg market. It begins at four in the morning and every vendor in the city is there by half past to get their goods. In addition to fruit and veg you can get suitcases with fake British pound notes taped under satin lining, illegally imported cigarettes by the trash bag, hash stuffed into the heads of dolls, and methadone on hawk.

Though Ian is no longer a heroin freak he can't quit the lifestyle. He works for the Hassan Brothers doing labor, delivering messages, and moderately abuses methadone by spiking his doses with whatever benzies are around, Valium, Xanax, Tranxene. The Hassan Brothers are four brothers who constitute the Pakistani mafia. They dominate the east side and control a third of the illegal activities at the fruit and veg market. Some nights Ian has to work. On those nights he drives the brothers in their van. At said location the brothers get out of the van with a baseball bat. Ian remains in the van, motor running. When the brothers return to the van the bat is bloody and all they want to do is snort coke and have sex with hookers. They get a room. The women have sex with each other then have sex with the brothers. Ian watches the door. These nights are called "Busting Caps" because

the first thing they do with the baseball bat is bash someone's kneecaps.

Once I say to Ian he should find a new gig. I say it while
eating dinner. Dinner is one of two things. Meat, pota-
toes, something out of a can, or: fried egg on a piece of
white bread with baked beans on top. The night I say it it
is meat/potatoes/something out of a can. Ian eats with
both hands, hunched at the plate like a dog. After I say it
he raises his head from his plate and looks at me. He says
nothing but he is holding his fork with his fist and the
fork trembles.

After that we stick to the dinner routine. Ian comments
on how fucking miserable Glasgow weather is. Yes, I say,
the weather is fucking miserable. Then I ask how his day
was. His day was always fine. He relays an episode from
his day, then asks how my day was: At market today this
shite wanker did so & so / how was your day. My day is
always fine. I do not talk to Ian about what I am working
on at University. I did once and then we didn't know
what to say to each other and it was weird.

After dinner Ian has his tea and examines a damaged
piece of paper on which he keeps a list of his bookie bets.
Sometimes he makes marks on the damaged paper with

a stubby pencil. After his tea he says: all right then that's me. He takes off his clothes and gets in bed. I like to see Ian take off his clothes. His skin is close to muscle. In the beginning I would undress. I would have pleasure and he would have pleasure. He would shower, then sleep.

· ◦ ◦

I hear the echo of my footsteps against cobble. It is late. Shops are closed and the streets are empty. I turn down a narrow alley. I walk and walk. Eventually I see a light coming from a door left ajar. I stop in front of the door. It is an old wooden one. I gently push it open, then stoop to enter a room. The room is empty but in its far corner there is a door leading to another room. The light in fact comes from this room. I walk to this door, through it, and into the lit room.

The floor is white square tiles and the walls are white. There is a stainless steel table and it is bright. A large man is in the room. He wears white pants, a white shirt, and an apron. There is blood on the apron and he holds a bone saw. He is butchering a cow that hangs from the ceiling. He is a butcher.

It is understood I am to watch. He is focused, slow, and skillful. He looks to me after he does something to make sure I have seen it. I nod my head to tell him yes, I have seen it. It takes him the whole night to butcher the cow. The rule is we will not speak and I will not leave until it is done.

It is a good dream. Thorough and quiet. I wake calmed. Throughout the day I hear a slight buzzing in my ears, but feel peaceful inside.

The dream repeats. Sometimes there are variations. I enter the room and the butcher will not be butchering a cow, but a pig. When there are variations I wake feeling unsettled at first, but soon after, peaceful.

One night I enter the room and he is not butchering a cow or pig but a child. A little boy. Lying on the floor in a hacked stack is another boy on top of a woman I know to be the mother of these children. The butcher works. Focused, slow, and skillful. It is still the rule that we will not speak and I will not leave until it is done.

After that I never know what I will find in the butcher's room. Sometimes a cow, sometimes a pig, sometimes a person. When it is a cow or pig I feel calm during the day. When it is a person I feel hysterical.

* * *

The last time Ian and I have sex it is late afternoon, light becoming dark. The trajectory began. Him on top [general pleasure]. Then it would go: me on top [making my own pleasure], him on top [conclusion: him making his own pleasure]. But something happened. It happened during general pleasure.

His body smoothly moving in. The sheet gathering under my skin. I felt my pelvis. Every in, it ground thin. The small of my back meeting mattress in sweat compressions. The coiled aches in the springs meeting seams. I felt the heaving weight of his body. The bone tips beneath the pressure. Him pitching through. I could see his face. Serious and blank. I could see his face and feel the complete weight of his body and I could feel my body taking it. Then something else happened.

There was a thought but I did not have it. It was had. I was the thought and was had. The thought was, *this is how it has always been.* This ancient position, a pattern. All at once my body was every woman that had ever been on her back until I felt into the body of the first woman. The original woman. On the cool floor of the garden. And what she thought: How one of the first things was this. Being on your back, being fucked.

Then I was above and waiting. We were waiting. While we waited we watched the silent picture show below. In it one of the bodies moved. It moved like an animal. The moving body moved.

The other body beneath the moving body also watched, was still, watching us watch, and its mouth drew a circle with its lips. The moving body gleamed in the room emptied of all but the slicking. The still body's mouth erupted. The abysmal sound of suctions hissing.

Eventually the stage emptied. A tangle of sheets, some crumbs. The theater filled with light becoming dark. Blue light. Night comes.

* * *

When I stop sleeping with Ian then stop sleeping it is noticed. It is different. Life continues. At night I sit in front of the terrible room's large bay window. I look out of it, smoke cigarettes, and think about shit.

Here, This Speck and This Speck
You Missed

I had been informed about Glasgow weather. Maybe in literature University sent before my arrival or maybe someone told me. I told myself the weather would not be like Mississippi, which was good.

In Glasgow it rains every day. Everything is always wet. Which was how it was in Mississippi. Except here wet is cold. In Mississippi wet is hot. I count thirty-seven days before a day in which there is no rain and some sun. On that day it is still cold but the sun is out and overall it is the warmest day anyone can ever remember. The city's entire population goes to City Park, men remove their shirts, thousands lie silently as beached whales.

I could only bring two suitcases on the transatlantic flight. In one, books I promptly sold at Barras Market for cigarettes and lager, and in the other, clothes. Since I didn't know what clothes to bring I tried to cover a few moods. A red dress for a cocktail party mood. Blue corduroy jeans for a student mood. Regular jeans and long-sleeved shirts for an everyday mood. With money I saved from being an Appointment Book Girl I bought two wool sweaters, a rain-coat, and waterproof boots. I forgot to pack the shoes that went with the red dress, which I trade at Barras for a small chunk of hash. It is a limited palette of clothes but I am clever with my combinations and know how to accessorize.

One morning after Ian leaves for work I take off my clothes and crawl into bed. I have not slept in five days. My mind wakes before my body and in those few moments I experience the quiet darkness of what sleep must be. It makes me weep. Which makes me open my eyes.

I must get out of bed and prepare to leave for the Postmodern happening. I must pull myself out and walk to University, then into the seminar room. I must sit next to others and might speak. We might speak. There is this list of actions and the weight of my body and I do not know how to push the list through.

Ian's clothes are piled on the floor. I pick up one of his old long-sleeved shirts. It is an Iron Maiden T-shirt that says POWERSLAVE across the front. I put it on. On top of that I put on one of his long-sleeved flannel button-ups. The shirts hang huge. I pull on jeans, boots, and leave. I guess that's when I first start dressing like a man.

* * *

Ian returns from work, opens the door, and sees me perched in the middle of the bed. I had the dream when it is a person and not a cow or pig.

After I woke I got out of bed to relieve a sick stomach and halfway to the toilet felt dizzy and leaned against the wall. A hand came out of the wall and touched me. I returned to bed. When Ian walks in the room I tell him about the hand in the wall through slobbering gasps of breath.

He walks to the bed and places his hands on my shoulders. He says it was a bad dream but I am O.K. now. He is kind and makes tea. He sits beside me on the bed while I drink the tea and talks about normal things to remind me of the world. How in the world Leeds won the football match and how in the world he saw a child who had got her head stuck between rail posts in the park and though it was sad it was funny.

My head is on his chest. His work boots are on and I don't care that they are in the bed. He puts his arm around me. I ask Ian if he thinks I'm crazy. Ian says he does not think I am crazy. He says it's life that's crazy.

*   *   *

I do not have many social obligations so this one fills me with anxiety. I meet Vivian at a pub in the University district.

Vivian is one of two remaining females at The Postmodern Seminar for the Study of Interpretive Uses. One finished her degree and the other dropped out to move to Champaign, Illinois where she works at the Estée Lauder counter in the mall and is having an affair with a youth minister. Vivian is from England and says her parents are far-out Anglicans even though they sound to me like Presbyterians. She is a prodigy and has been invited into the seminar as its youngest member.

The meeting does not go well. I do not know any of the DJs everyone knows. I do not know what a bubble tea is and sound weird when I order one because she has one and assumes I will. My research bores her and she takes an incoming call. Remembering people love to talk about themselves, which can be a way to get them to like you, I ask about her research. After her degree she will begin her graduate studies directly. She knows what her graduate thesis will be and how she will prove it. It will be apocalyptic landscapes in twentieth-century literature and she will prove it with Kant. She is petite with long curly red hair and leather pants.

I want to connect to Vivian. There must be a common thread. We are women. There are few women in the program where it is not easy to be a woman. Many of our habits are the same. These are the habits of animals. But there is no connection with Vivian.

That afternoon a window had to be closed in the seminar room because it is too cold. Vivian jumps on top of the seminar table. With her slight frame and scholarly but still punk rock look she leans toward the large window and yanks it down. She pops off the table, back into her seat. It is an extraordinary thirty seconds. Though she just closed a window it was as if she had slid down a fireman's pole or performed Kung Fu.

I have a feeling. It is hard to say what it is and I do not know if it is mine or if it comes from others in the room. The feeling is: She's the Ideal Academic Girl. The feeling is: this extraordinary tabletop move is who we are.

People have to take turns leading seminar happenings and that day it is Gay Irish Danny's turn. Gay Irish Danny talks about the Physical and the Sensual in gay Irish poetry. The room sighs. Gay Irish Danny delivers his monologue in a brave voice and everyone practices tolerance. Between not understanding his theoretical terms, being grossly underread, and being bored shitless, I think about how Gay Irish Danny has managed to make gay sex as unhot as humanly possible.

After, the conversation turns to Derrida and Gay Irish Danny makes a question out of it in terms of how a woman's perspective would be different. Wow, I think, that's a good question. The room sighs. Gay Irish Danny asks me in particular what I think about the question. I say I think it is a good question. He keeps looking at me like I'm supposed to say something else. But I do not have anything else to say. He gets an awkward look on his face and the conversation returns to Derrida.

After seminar I return to the terrible room. I take a pair of scissors and cut my long hair in random chunks until it is short. I accidentally snip my ears and there are thin lines of blood on my cheeks. Looking at myself I think it is the hair of someone in a train wreck, something about it.

I go to the corner barber and hope he doesn't say anything, just does it, which is how it goes. He shaves away what is left.

A man ate a bicycle. He worked at a fish & chips shop. He was quiet, had a mustache, a little overweight. The girl behind the counter at the fish & chips shop says: nice because he was there but you know not.

Think of it, eating an entire bicycle. A Schwinn Shimano 3-speed with a Stingray Gripper Slik back, an iridescent blue aluminum frame, liner-pull pedals, brakes perched like doves in the crook of curved handlebars, vinyl grip-taped.

Some parts of the bicycle could be swallowed as plunking a penny in a well. But others like the chainwheel would have to be let. Lowered through upward rippling esophagus, sprockets snatching linings, eviscerating the passages, until cavities jam, then fist knocked, in. Other parts like the alloy kickstand would require the entire body for acceptance, a slow-motion robot dance. He didn't eat it all at once. That would be crazy. He ate through time. At the hospital when technicians see the x-rays they spit their tea. Word gets out and in the local papers. He was the guy who ate an entire bicycle.

Why did he do it? I ask Ruth and Ian. They think it's hilarious a guy would eat a bicycle, but why? Did he eat a bicycle so we don't have to? Maybe God sent a man who eats bicycles. He was probably mentally ill but is mental illness a disqualifier in the realm of men sent from God? We don't know that it is. We can't say there is a God. The I-just-know-in-my-heart feeling could be impure. It could be confused with something darkly sexual, for example. Don't you think it's tragic that a man would eat a bicycle? It's a lonely thing to do.

I think the man thought if he ate the bicycle he would save himself from spontaneous human combustion. The heel-licking threat of disappearance. I think he thought if he ate the bicycle he could stay. Ruth and Ian laugh and Ruth splashes half her pint she laughs so hard.

That night I sit in front of the bay window, and in my head I say to Ruth and Ian that when you hear a story about a man eating a bicycle it's like hearing a story you already know, it is impossible, but isn't. I say: May the story of the man who ate a bicycle be a lesson to you.

And Suddenly I Thought:
This Is What It Means to Make
a Movie in Sweden

The Postmodern Seminar for the Study of Interpretive Uses decides to include film as text. We gather two nights a month, watch movies, and drink scotch though never enough.

After one film I get in a fight with a master's candidate from Washington, DC who is doing his last year of research at the Seminar by invitation. At a departmental gathering to welcome new students he once reprimanded a Theoretical Studies girl for using "Heidegger" and "grace" in the same sentence. Never use the word "grace" he said. It shows your hand. By which he meant ass. He said it like her use of "grace" revealed her trailer park origins when she should try and marry better. Oh, said the Theoretical Studies girl, scribbling a note to herself on a napkin.

The film we got in a fight about ended with a woman being killed by a soldier. She was pretty much dead but he did her in for good by jamming a gun in her vagina then pulling the trigger. The film didn't show this but implied it. The question the fight hinged on was this: Did the woman, in the last split second of her life, experience the meaning of her suffering? Washington said yes. The possibility of experiencing such meaning, despite solitude and cruelty, was the rule.

I thought this was a romantic view of what the last split second of life might be like. And I thought it was unfair. It was stealing the woman's death from her, which meant in the end everything was taken. Taken and put in the ghettos of our intellectualizations. Soured thoughts counting more than smears of blood. Why couldn't we sit in the pain of not knowing? Maybe she didn't get the big meaning of her suffering. Maybe she just suffered, then died.

When the fight is finally drawn to a close by the head of the Seminar, Washington has won because he is smart and uses language like an exacto blade. He never raised his voice and has remained calm. My face is red and my voice shaky. As people leave the room they look at me like they feel sorry for me and look at Washington like he is a great guy who understands theology.

Later, I look out of the terrible room's bay window. In my head I say to the people who watch movies that it is a stretch to think that the witness knows what it is like to die. I say: May the story of Washington, DC be a lesson to you.

*　*　*

Feaking heil whut youd do yrself, says Ruth, touching the stubble. I am sitting in a chair and Ruth is standing, one hand on one hip, the other holding a cigarette poised inches from her face. She is looking at me, amused and horrified by my shaven head. Well then that's you, she says.

She tucks a towel around my shoulders and mixes the solution. Hair bleach in Scotland is different from hair bleach in the States. It is purchased from the chemist and the box it comes in is dusty and pink with movie star script that says Fanci-Faux Lady.

Having extremely short hair means it is easier to bleach. But it burns more. Ruth says it is because my head is like a baby's bum, all brand new. It burns so much I don't know if I can take it. I consider running for the shower. But if I washed it off then my hair would not be blond and I would have to repeat the process so I will sit for the half hour the solution requires.

Ruth goes to the corner shop to get a fifth of something. I am glad to be left alone. If my head were not on fire it would be a lovely day. The sun has come out and though cold, the window can be raised a little to let in fresh air.

Across from my building is another exactly like it. Exactly where my bay window is, its bay window is. It has one sagging curtain permanently pulled back. No one lives in the building.

I cannot help the tears streaming down my face. They are an automatic response to the intensity of the burning. I use the opposite room that mirrors my room as a focal point to ride through the pain and the pain sharpens my ability to focus and I can see into the room. I have never been able to before but now I see how rose-printed paper peels from the walls in drooping sheets. There is a bureau in the room and its top drawer is open. In front of the window is a chair. The chair is just like my chair.

I open my mouth and hear a sound. I am surprised then realize the sound comes from inside me. It is low and sustained, like it has a motor in the middle of it. When I close my mouth the sound stops. When I open my mouth it begins. I decide to open my mouth. I open it all the way. The room fills with the drone of bees. I close my mouth. The sound continues.

* * *

Barras Market is medieval meat market turned modern-day kasbah. Tourists are cautioned against Barras since most will be robbed or otherwise humiliated. You can get anything at Barras, mostly crap, and if you're into butchers it's a month of Sundays. It's where I get cigarettes, hash, and old photographs for five pence apiece. For Ruth's birthday I give her one of a baby dressed like a pope. On the back it says: Birdie's Last Easter. Even though it's now a regular market butchers still work in open air. They have their blocks and scales.

The butchers wear red-and-white striped paper caps to indicate their trade. They hack the meat, weigh it, and the crowd bids. The butcher curses the crowd for being no-good cheap bastards. He waves the meat above his head and curses. The remainder of the carcass is covered in flies and sits by the scale in pools of pink watered-down blood dripping to the ground. When a piece is sold the butcher wraps it in newspaper and takes the money with bloody dirty hands.

Ian, Ruth, and I stand in the butcher's crowd but the butcher knows we are not buying but watching. Eventually he tells us to fuck off. It's a ritual. It's the first thing we do at Barras before getting high.

* * *

Students may use University health club for free. Inside are many who know where to go and what to do. They have outfits. I wear a gray sweatsuit resembling Ken's I got from a charity shop that sold stuff to save Africa. At the health club I go for one of the classes since I am afraid of the machines and the people who use them. I choose aerobics. Though I have never attended an aerobics class I have an idea of what one is.

Aerobics is held in the health club's inside basketball court. From the court you can look up and see the people on machines behind a wall of glass. The people on machines look down upon the people on the basketball court doing aerobics.

A muscular guy stands in the middle of the court and blows a whistle. After he blows the whistle he shouts: run. People begin to run around the perimeter of the basketball court. He keeps shouting and seems angry with us. Techno music blares. Every few minutes he blows the whistle. Then everyone turns and runs in the opposite direction. These transitions are never smooth.

There is one guy in aerobics who stands out a) because he's the only guy other than the instructor and b) he's the only really thin person in aerobics. He is anorexic. He is a running skeleton but his face is fleshy, swollen. He has an excited look on his face like he is going to follow orders when the drill sergeant says fucking run. When I notice him I am alarmed. Do they know he is in aerobics? Someone should stop him. He is dying right in front of us.

Aerobics isn't what I thought it was. After three classes I never return to University health club. I think about square dancing with Rorrie. What happened to him. What happened to all those people.

*   *   *

I tell Ian I think I could do it, I think I could slaughter a cow. Thinking it and doing it are two different things, he says. I think I could, I say, I think I could for real. Maybe, Ian says, you should just learn to bloody cook it.

I don't tell Ian how much I really know. How to first open the carcass and remove the entrails inside the chest cavity using a boning knife. Slowly. As to not puncture vital organs. How to then split the hide back to rear with a bone saw in order to efficiently cut open the tailbone to remove the rest of the entrails. How to see-saw the blade up, halving the upper chest cavity. How to flush the cavity of the carcass with clear and cold water and dry the cavity with thin white towels. How now the slaughter is ready for hanging.

Hang the rear legs high. Remove any remaining hide using the thin blade of a skinning knife. With the bone saw in one hand, grab the head with the other. Saw it off. Angle the bone saw into the front legs and saw and saw. With a boning knife, a skinning knife, and butchering knife, hack and carve. Down to rounds. Rump, loin, plate, rib, chuck, and shank.

❋ ❋ ❋

My favorite movie at Seminar Movie Night is *The Seventh Seal* by Ingmar Bergman. In the movie, times are terrible.

It takes place when people are figuring out the Crusades were pointless and the plague is killing everyone in Europe. In the movie the Knight Antonius Block plays a chess game with Death. Everything that happens in the story is part of the game then the game ends. Death wins the game.

After the movie I find a book at University library that has Ingmar Bergman's screenplays along with movie pictures. I photocopy a picture of Antonius Block and Death.

In the picture they sit across from one another, a chessboard between them. It is either sunrise or sunset. In the background, dramatic clouds and the sea. Antonius Block's hand hovers above the chessboard. Light hits his face and knuckles and the rest of him is in shadow though you can tell he is reclining against a rock. He has an amused look on his face. Sitting opposite, Death. Death has good posture and leans forward with a slight but not unfriendly smile.

It looks so conversational. It's funny to see the Dark Lord of the Underworld sitting down. What is funny is that Death can sit down. If he sits maybe he does other normal things. I like the idea you could be halfway to hell and Death would have to stop and go to the bathroom.

And it's all so straightforward. Death looks like the popular renderings. Everyone knows who he is. You never know when he is going to come but when he does it's how a person comes. If you're in a tree he walks up with an axe and cuts it down in real time. If you're eating dinner he knocks on the door and has to walk all the way through the house to get to the dining room where you sit with your soup bowl. He has to get down in the pits and pull out the half-dead bodies himself. The agony of dying is seeing Death actually approach as a very large man with a black cowl that is too tight around his face.

I think it would be the greatest thing if Death would be like he was in the olden days. I like to imagine Death marching through crowded streets, riding the subway, and entering the shops.

I do not think if Death was a large man we could see that it would make us less ridiculous or keep us more honest.

I do not know why I long to see Death this way. I love the picture and take it everywhere though I never show it to anyone.

Aboard, My Love!
The Sun Is a Profound Gamble:
Another Day and Still Another

I have never seen a Russian Palace but think the Glasgow Museum looks like one. It is fantastically large, dim, and broken. Crammed with many inconsequential works, it also has a Bug Room. Its exhibits empty except for decaying black habitats. The Bee Colony is the only working exhibit and it doesn't work. The bees are housed in a plexiglass tank. The tank has a slender tube leading to a hole that opens outside the museum so the bees can leave the colony then come back just like in a real bee colony. Hundreds of dead gooey bees jam the slender tube blocking the exit in clumps. The remainder of trapped bees fly erratically into the plexiglass walls of the tank.

Down the hall from the Bug Room is the Red Room. In the Red Room hangs Rembrandt's *Study for a Slaughtered Ox*. There is a bench in front of the painting. At first I sit in front of it instead of attending The Postmodern Seminar for the Study of Interpretive Uses. Then I sit in front of it when I'm supposed to be at University library writing my research thesis.

I love the painting. It looks like a lot of things other than just a slaughtered ox. It looks like a bed sheet with sex blood, a war bandage show-and-tell, a crucifixion, and an open book. The painting is set up so you're outside the painting looking at it but at the same time you are in the room of the painting. Rembrandt painted it so that the two rooms would be the same room. In the painting it's like something was there, then wasn't. Notably missing, the butcher. Where is he? You can see the room is empty. Except it's not. You are there.

I create a shorthand to map the complex spatial relations between the *Slaughtered Ox* and every other work of art in the museum, including the stuff in the Armor Room with its fake horses, including the bees.

After I finish the map I must constantly make adjustments but am able to take my research to the next level. I catalogue information regarding how people react to the *Slaughtered Ox*. Usually it is the random tourist driven into the museum by foul weather. Either people make a stupid face because they do not know what to make of a hung picture of hung slaughter in a room showcasing bland Cornish ceramics or they move on, bored.

The information I glean comes from the space between the viewer's body and the painting. I have to glean by listening at the inverted arc of the body countercurrent to its fluttering capillaries. I do not know what this information means but I record what I hear.

When Ian asks how my day was I say fine and do not tell him I have been sitting in front of the *Slaughtered Ox*. When I go to the museum I try and look official like an art history student or something. When an attendant approaches to ask if I'm O.K. and sees my cut-up hands it is difficult to continue comforting myself with the thought that I appear to belong. On the days overriding museum staff feels like too much I go to the Botanical Gardens where I can sit inside a big bubble building and look at tropical plants. At the Botanical Gardens I make lists of things I will do.

Before I put anything on the list I imagine everything that thing involves. I put Make A Quilt on the list but first make it in my mind. It takes a long time to make a quilt. I put Read Everything Freud Wrote and Become A Girl Scout Leader. It takes almost two weeks to imagine reading everything Freud wrote. Meanwhile in Girl Scouts we invent new badges. There will be, for example, a Poetry Badge.

* * *

I put one hand on my stomach and one on my lower back. The space between my hands is the middle. I look in the mirror. The image in the mirror looks. One of its hands is on its front and one is on its back. Between its hands is the middle.

I press the hand on my stomach in and I press the hand on my back in. The hands do not touch but could come close. The middle space between front and back is not much. Yet it connects the front and back. I look in the mirror and it is confirmed by the image. The middle space does connect front and back. The middle are the insides. The insides come between front and back and connect them. I see it is not much.

But know it is much more. A space so far across that front and back are not seen at once and could not touch. The me that looks in the mirror and the image in the mirror that looks has one hand on its front and one hand on its back. They almost touch. I see but it is not seen. A trick of seeing seen. Where is it. What is. Is not in mirrors.

Mochè the drunk is withered, his dirty face the color of tobacco leaves. He wears khaki pants held around his puffed gut by an old leather belt. Sometimes shirt, sometimes not. His chest hair is wiry, white, and sporadic. His head hair is gray dreadlocks and he smells like piss.

Most of the time Mochè is so gone he's not on this planet. He sits on the foyer bench with a bottle of sherry. Ken gets Mochè's monthly check, takes what he wants, then gives Mochè enough to stay wasted until the next check comes. Mochè has been living at Red Pepper Station for five years.

At the pub Ruth says she guesses she'd be that fucked too if she was him. Mochè is a Jew and his family got killed in the war. She says the stain on his wrist is a number the Nazis put there. Before the war Mochè's father owned a pantyhose factory in Warsaw and they were rich.

On New Year's Ian works so I make a plate of food and take it to Mochè. I knock on his door and he opens it. I made you some food, I say. He looks at the fried egg smothered in baked beans. A cigarette hangs from his mouth. He asks if I want a drink. Mochè brings me a coffee mug of sherry. He drinks from the bottle. He doesn't eat the food. We sit in metal folding chairs in his bedsit. Other than the folding chairs there is a mattress.

He asks if I'm religious since a holiday just passed. No, I say. Me neither, he says. I know, I say, You're a Jew. We don't have anything else to say so I ask him about the Holocaust. How long were you in the Holocaust, I ask. He takes a swig of sherry and laughs, the fatty crescents under his arms jiggling.

I take Mochè baked beans smothering a fried egg once a week and he never eats it. I bring my own booze since I can't deal with sherry and feel weird about drinking his since I know it's all he's got. It's how I learn about the Polish pantyhose industry.

Do you think you'd be a drunk if it weren't for the Holocaust, I ask. Yes, he says. I think I would.

Sometimes there are lulls in our conversations. It is in a lull when I tell him about these guys I used to know. I say: I use to know these guys.

What about these guys, Mochè says. I hold my drink between my legs and my face screws up. Mochè pours me another, his trembling hand, and we sit in the metal folding chairs.

Inside there is a thing. It is buoyant. It bounces on top of an organ located above the navel. I do not know what organ this would be but know it to be pink. Not pink of a girl's room or roses, rather the salamander thick of institutional lunches. The thing must sit on the pink organ or float above it. But when bouncing it rises between rib bones. This upper stratosphere of clear is not used to foreign objects so it burns. The burning curls edges, which splits the cinder stitches. The chest opens. Gasp. Breath is a hammer coming down.

* * *

At University library I learn the only officially recorded Dutch animal paintings of the mid- to late-1600s were "a bass" sold by the physician Johannes Dillemas in 1662 and "a painting with a dog" known to be in the collection of Joris van Corshot in 1671. Other than these two authenticated works, art documentation of the period notes two other possible legitimate references to paintings featuring animals, in 1640 and 1665 respectively, though few details are known. During this same period there are three references concerning two animal paintings done by Rembrandt, however these references have been omitted from the cannon of academic classification.

In 1656 an ox painting by Rembrandt is located in an "anteroom to an art gallery in a house" along with a painting by Titus, described as "a book." It is conjectured Titus began the still life but did not complete it. It is suggested Rembrandt completed the book begun by Titus.

In 1661 a "painting depicting a slaughtered ox by Rembrandt" was in the ownership of the Nurnberger, Christoffel Hirschovogel. Two days before leaving Amsterdam he told the man with whom he was leaving his belongings, the lawyer Theodroe Ketjens, that the Rembrandt was worth seventy-five guilders. After his departure Ketjens had it appraised at no higher than thirty.

In 1681 the artist Michiel van Coxie met Wybrand de Geest II. Geest, a Fristian, was the relative of Gerrit Uylenburgh who traded art and also patroned Coxie. During their meeting the artist claimed to own "an ox by Rembrandt."

In the late nineteenth century an academic synod concluded Rembrandt could not have been involved with the production of the ox paintings otherwise they would be famous and they weren't. It is suggested that these works, if in fact done by Rembrandt, were painted over by an associate so that something of Rembrandt was within the slaughtered ox, but bastardized beyond paternity as a result. Rembrandt's last work before his death was a self-portrait. He poses as Zarathustra, the mythic figure who died laughing.

Inside——   The chest opens. Gasp. Breath is a hammer coming down. A blank white flashes. Left. Left right left. The thing gathers speed bouncing up and when it returns to the pink organ it otherwise floats above or rests upon it, lands on the organ's bruised top. Repetition has bruised the organ. The tender organ has become more supple, bashed.

The throb's mainline drops tentacles. The tentacles have stingers at tipped ends that stun the outer walls of a tract. A ribbon of electrocution widens vagina, darts into ass as stab. Made by little fists holding little knives. The brassy echo of stabbing heard in inner ears. White blanking. Left. Left right left.

The stabs find their rhythm and every third wave reverses the direction of a small hard filament, which enters a small hole located at the bottom of the organ. The filament pushes through the organ's webbing. The webbing does not delay the filament with tiny net-like hairs, the filament is self-motivating and travels up and through approaching the hole on top of the organ, which is a spout that spits it out.

As the filament exits, it creates energy. The energy causes the thing above the organ to bounce. The thing rises into the burning stratosphere between rib bones and the filament floats to the bottom where waves of stabbing collect and send it off again.

Outside—   A woman in bed sheets, face down. Her limbs curl to center pulled by blue slackless inner chords. The center is soft, feverish, stomach. She draws knees up, one at a time. Left. Left right left. Then pushes them back down, one at a time. Left. Left right left. Arms at elbows bend, casing flanks, pinned.

The horizontal climbing unclothes her. Shirt offing, underwear offing. She writhes into her nakedness. In measured beats her body stiffens, rises, then lands again. The burning thing inside is tied tight at one end by a string. A yellow hand pulls it through. Left. Left right left. It opens her mouth. Out come moans. Her rib bones are the infrastructure of a well that tunnels to the heart of the earth. She falls into it.

So that is what it was for.

Days following the pain, stomach walls are quicksand. When food is again eaten it comes out immediately. I may as well eat on the toilet. In the beginning it came out soft and awful, like baby shit. Later, as water that cuts.

Sitting at the pub, Ruth, Ian, and I wonder what it is. Perhaps a stomach ulcer. The burning star inside the guts of dumpy men who work in offices. Ruth says perhaps flu, her face like a mother's. After all I am puking and shitting my brains out.

Since aerobics isn't what I thought I decide I will walk fast. I will do it very early in the morning because I do not want to be observed by people. The Kelvin River winds through the middle of the city. There is a path beside it and this is where I will do it.

There's crap in the river and around the river. There are also ducks and swans. I like the swans. They are filthy but still look like swans. In the dense fog of early morning I like to see them silently sailing between the banks of glittering trash.

The path sticks to the river with few exceptions. One exception is a mile from the Botanical Gardens. In the distance you can see the Maryhill projects that became inundated after the Gorbal slums were torn down because of rat infestations. When you pass Maryhill there is another half mile before you hook up with the river again. This is where the old playground is.

You can tell kids haven't used the playground in years. Weeds have overtaken and it has the unsafe look some playgrounds have before people gave more of a shit about child safety. There is a dangerous jungle gym, a tall and narrow slide with thin broken steps, some chain-length swings, and one of those springy riding things. The springy riding thing has a large thick coil rooted in a concrete stump partially set in the ground. A kid would sit on the plastic animal atop the spring and pretend to ride it. The animal atop this spring is hard to identify. It was once white with red spots and appears to be half horse, half seal. The horseseal's body is bent forward so that its head touches the ground with a frightening upside-down smile.

The fog is thick and I can't see ten feet in front of me so I sit on the playground's bench and have a smoke. Sharp edges of eroding playground equipment poke through the still blanket of fog. I finish my smoke but don't leave. I roll another.

I wonder if I'll ever finish my thesis. I wonder what will happen to Ian. I wonder if he'll make it. I hope he makes it. I wonder about Ruth. Ruth feels in transition but never goes anywhere. I think about cancer. I wonder if Ruth will get cancer. I think about Mochè, how he shakes, the old leather belt, and his puffed gut. I wonder about the pain I now feel almost every day. It feels like a hot knife writing my name in cursive. I feel something that may be my childhood. It is a gray shelf inside me. I think about my mother and sister. I miss them. Where did they go. What happened to them.

Eee awwl eee awwl. My skin goes cold. Eee awwl eee awwl. The sound is a rusty knuckle grating a chain at the joint. A swing on the swing set is swinging. Walking fast isn't what I thought it was.

*　*　*

It's an old story.

Mutual poverty brings two women together. One is old, a worn-out hag. One is young with no prospects of marriage. By day they clean houses. By night, by strained eye, they stitch the clothing of strangers in an oil-lamp-lit shack. Then a miracle happens. Beyond childbearing years, the hag gives birth to a golden baby boy. The young woman looks at the exhausted, still panting hag. And she thinks. She thinks about how things are. How her young body is fruit on the vine, how since she has no dowry and won't marry well, any man who might eat of it will be oafish and stupid. The woman lifts the child from the birth mess between the hag's legs. This baby's mine, she says.

She takes the child to the cathedral and holds him for all to see. To the crowd she says, A miracle has happened. God favored me and I have delivered this golden child. An excited murmur runs through the crowd. Most know the young woman. None recall she was pregnant or admits to laying with her. It is a miracle.

The crowd gathers. The child is content and does not cry. He does have a wise expression on his face. Women touch his perfect feet then swoon. A man touches the child's head and is cured of gout. Word spreads.

The Archbishop of the cathedral, an evil, ambitious, and handsome young man, sees the effect the child has. Goddamn it, he thinks. Since he must appease the vulgarity of the masses, he decides it is better for this situation to be incorporated into the Church so it can be controlled.

The woman is given beautiful gowns of silk and the child is dressed in linen suits made by nimble-fingered nuns. The woman and child sit on a special throne within the cathedral. Pilgrimages are made throughout the kingdom to receive the blessing of the child.

Things start to look up for the previously depressed town. The inns are full of pilgrims, which means the taverns are full at night. Town women bake special Golden Child Cakes and sell them to the scores of people who wait to enter the Cathedral. The town's children dress like animals and perform skits for the crowds and raise enough money to build a community theater.

And though it put the Cathedral on the map, so to speak, still the Archbishop's heart was dark. Years of self-sacrifice and enduring various humiliations when, in an instant, some tramp could get off and what is worse, profit by it.

When the final pilgrim left the Cathedral for the day the Archbishop slipped from behind the shadows, for he often hid in the shadows and watched the woman, how she gingerly placed the child on her knee and bounced her knee which caused her décolleté to bounce thus its fragrance wafting into the pitch of his hiding place. Hello Arnaud, she said without turning to face him, for the woman called the Archbishop by his first name whenever she liked. Goddamn it, he thought.

I've been thinking, she said. I think the miracle baby would like a grander house. And he should like his mother to take the healing Cornish waters on holiday for a fortnight. And he should like it if salted butter were at every meal. And wine. He should like it if there were wine. The Archbishop felt his heart constrict. I think not, said the Archbishop. I see, said the woman. In that case perhaps I should call on your old friend, Jean Claude, Bishop of Arles. For I have been thinking the lowlands irritate the baby's sinuses, that a change of climate, perhaps a less moist cathedral for example, would do his constitution good.

Jean Claude of Arles, arch-nemesis of the Archbishop. How well that insipid bastard would rub his thumbs together and grin were that many-breasted harlot to move her horse and pony show. The woman moved into a grander house, her meals improved, and there was no shortage of wine. She took fabulous, exotic holidays.

On the Feast Day of St. Martin the Archbishop enters the packed Cathedral in finest regalia, staff included, which he usually saved for Christmas. Behind him, ten armed guards.

Hear ye! the Archbishop says in his Christmas dress, dramatically raising his staff. The crowd stops talking amongst themselves and looks to the Archbishop. This woman is a fraud! he yells, How she has fooled you, this patron of Satan. This whore bride of Lucifer! The woman watches the Archbishop from her throne, bouncing the baby faster and faster upon her knee.

This woman did not give birth to this baby! the Archbishop yells with an excited look on his face. He'd been doing his homework and found out about the old hag, etc. The guards shackle the woman and take the baby. An astonished gasp runs through the crowd.

Since the woman has committed several mortal sins she must die according to Church law but Church law also clearly states you cannot hang a virgin which technically the woman still is. A judicial committee is formed, headed by the Archbishop, and a resolution is quickly found. The Archbishop sends four horsemen each with a letter bearing his seal to the four corners of the kingdom. The crowds come in droves. The inns are full, thus the taverns. Women sell delicious baked goods to the long lines. The community theater produces a stunning rendition of Thornton Wilder's *Our Town.*

The woman is bound to four posts of a four-poster bed. The bed sits on a specially made platform and is surrounded by a translucent tent lit inside by candles. Every time a man enters the tent a guard stationed in front of the tent tears a blank page from a large book and holds it above a spear, centering the spear's tip beneath the page. When the man exits the tent the guard thrusts the paper through the spear.

There are a thousand pages in the blank book, which represents the Book of Life in Revelations, the book of Revelations, which says, "Since in her heart she says, 'A queen I sit, I am no widow, mourning I shall never see,' so shall her plagues come in a single day." After a thousand sex acts she'll hardly be a virgin. But there is no need to hang the woman. She dies halfway through the book.

It's an old story, in fact, a passion play popular during medieval times when it was often performed in front of churches. After it is performed at University I walk the long way home even though it is raining. For the first time in a year I get in bed and sleep the night through. Thus it was that my insomnia was, for a little while, cured.

There Is a Host
in Ghost

I think of the bread on the table. It takes a half hour to slide out of bed and, face to floor, scoot toward the table and its bread using anklebones as pivoting pushers. When I get the bread I fold a whole piece into my mouth. Between hammer breaths and with the force of my mind I will it into my stomach. Thirty minutes later the pain stops. When I look in the bathroom mirror my face is crosshatched in scarlet carpet burns.

Perhaps this pain responds best to irony. Because for days after I will not be able to hold food maybe food is the cure. But how did the bread work? It absorbed the burning like a sacrificial victim. Like the demon in *The Exorcist* that jumped from the head-spinning body of the kid into the old priest who flew out a window. Funny since in my normal life I cannot eat bread and the day I stopped eating it was June, the sixth month, on the sixth, during the sixth year of my life. That day I was in my grandmother's just-painted kitchen. As a result of the thick fumes and heat I vomited the white bread mayonnaise bologna sandwich I was eating then swore off bread, mayonnaise, bologna, and every white food I could think of since the fragmented bread was white in white vomit.

After the piece of bread has a positive effect I put a loaf by the bed and wait. The next time the pain comes I eat a piece.

I add another ingredient. A big gulp of Pepto a few minutes after willing the bread down. The Pepto makes puke amidst pain. This gets the bread-slash-sacrificial-victim out quicker. Though I cannot be sure of the effect this purgative quality has, it seems to make the pain time shorten.

I add some other things. At onset of pain before bread followed by Pepto then puke, I insert a tampon. The cotton batting absorbs the lower sonar frequencies of refraction that illuminate the blackened interior in bright hair-thin constellations.

After the tampon, the bread, the Pepto, and the puking, I add a dash of Ian's methadone. Eating the methadone wafer makes my head shake left to right. Without the aid of Valium, Xanax, or some other pill it is not possible to achieve a buzz from methadone and I do not know why my head shakes left to right. If my head shakes too fast and pulls my chest along in the left-right motion, that's not good as it produces a midsection twisting that mirrors the pain instead of working contra to it by giving it a reverse image of itself, which is key.

When the head shaking left-right-left happens at the correct speed it frees the pained middle zone to resolve itself by imploding into a single efficient pinpoint so it can be captured. The inner eye can hardly perceive it but I focus on the darting with such keening it finally slows and can be seen as a still, single silver needle. Then it disappears.

Insert tampon, eat a piece of white bread, gulp Pepto, puke, have a bit of methadone, see the silver needle. It works if you work it.

When Ken said I had a call I was so excited someone should phone I jumped up like a contestant on *The Price Is Right*. I was glad to leave the room since Ian's childhood friend Fuckface Clive was visiting. Fuckface Clive only came around when he wanted to shoot speed. Ian and Fuckface Clive hated each other and I didn't understand why they liked to do speed together then remembered why. They hated each other. Fuckface Clive was a real comedian. He had a tattoo of Jesus on his left forearm and before he would shoot he'd tap his tattoo and say: Jesus on the main line. He also told jokes. Why did the feminist cross the road? To suck my dick.

Hello Baby is a bowl that comes out of my sister's mouth. There is static in the connection I imagine as bits of electrical but powdery dust. I know something is wrong. My sister has never phoned overseas or gotten in touch at all and Ken never lets anyone use his phone.

Baby I have some bad news, she says. I brace myself for what I know is my mother's death. How did it happen, I say. Do you think you can come, she asks. How did it happen, I say. What about a flight, can you get one.

I know there is no money for a flight. Yes, I say. I'm coming. I'm leaving this shithole and coming home.

Ian gets the flight money and I don't ask how. I give him a floppy disc in return. He is to take it with a handwritten note to University and give it to the department secretary who will print what is on the disc and give it to the dean. On the disc are my completed remaining degree requirements and my research thesis. In the end I will receive a paper and it will say I have a University degree in Religion.

* * *

When the lines straighten, pain. Blinding before captured. One does not want to *push through;* one fears still-
ness. The old ether through the meat story. The how to
get the egg through the iron wall one. If only If not but
then. If the medicine would begin [before the choking].

* * *

She got too high on coke then died, that's how. My sister and I pick out the cheapest box, which is pine. Standing at the grave we watch two men put the box in the ground. I read a poem Auden wrote after William Yeats died then my sister and I stand there. She is pregnant in a black leather miniskirt holding a pink carnation she will drop on the box that is in the ground. I am wearing a Metallica T-shirt, jeans, and a baseball cap, and am holding a cigarette I will accidentally drop on the tarp beside the box shape cut into the ground.

My sister suddenly gets an urgent look on her face. Who was William Yeats, she asks. A poet, I say. I liked the part toward the end, she says. Yeah, I say, that part's pretty good.

Follow, poet, follow right
to the bottom of the night.

IV

Magic Tricks for a Hospital Setting

The Disappearing Card Trick

The Disappearing Card Trick

Without access to my medicinal combination the pain becomes more intense and my sister gets freaked out. I tell her I will not go to the hospital then she cries. It is a relief for both of us when I go to the hospital.

At the hospital it is discerned I am malnourished, underweight, and dehydrated. I have slight internal bleeding, my blood pressure is extremely low, and some organs are in shock. I have a fever.

They do an ultrasound and blood tests. The blood tests reveal something called lipase and amylase are more than three times normal levels. A short man with an eye twitch orders a CT scan. The man is Dr. Moss and after he sees the test results he says I will have surgery and soon. He will perform the surgery in two day's time.

In surgery he will remove gallstones, repair an obstructed bile duct that connects to my liver, and remove some fluid-filled cysts. So that's the problem. No, he says, that's not the problem. That's an issue created by another problem. He asks if I know what a pancreas is.

A pancreas is a small organ located near the lower part of the stomach at the opening of the small intestine. It has two main functions. As an exocrine organ it produces digestive enzymes and as an endocrine organ it produces hormones, insulin being the most important. Through a system of ducts, the pancreas secretes digestive enzymes into the digestive tract. Meanwhile it secretes a variety of hormones directly into the bloodstream. Oh, I say. A nurse comes in the room and says I'll feel a stick. She hooks up a drip and a cold thump enters my vein. You have abnormal pancreatic function, he says, it's a chronic situation. This organ's inflammation and inability to function properly has damaged nearby tissue. Why don't you lay down, he says. The nurse puts a mask on my face. That's oxygen, he says. You have hypoxia, do you know what that is. I shake no. It means your body's cells are not receiving enough oxygen. The nurse injects a fat shot into the drip. That's morphine, he says. Although rare complications can be fatal. In such cases lung, kidney, and heart failure may all occur. The nurse puts a clipboard in my hands. Sign by the x, he says.

So, he says, here's the real question. Do you like magic?
Yes, I say through the mask. Well how about this, he says.

He pulls out two cards and moves them around fast.
What do you think about that, he says. What, I say. The
card trick. Oh, I say, yeah, it's cool. Do you know what
they call it, he asks. The disappearing card trick, I say.
No, he says. But he does not tell me the real name of the
trick then a nurse whisks him away.

* * *

I am admitted into the hospital and for the days prior to surgery. I am not to eat and am to take morphine. After taking morphine continuously through my drip it begins to burn the inside of my veins. My arms race with liquid fire banishing the happiness I initially felt about getting to take morphine for health purposes. My sister calls Ken's office and leaves a message for Ian to call me in the hospital. He calls the night before surgery.

His voice sounds far away and small. Well that's you then, he says. Yeah, I say. Do you need anything from here? Like what, I say. I dunno, he says. Like a book or something. No, I say, I don't feel like reading. How are things there? I ask. Well, he says, that's me, bloody fucking expensive phone call. Yeah, I say. Have your sis phone if something goes wrong, he says. Before we say good-bye I tell Ian to tell Ruth that I love her. When I say this it embarrasses us both. All right then. I never talk to Ian again.

Before surgery my sister rolls me outside so I can have a smoke. When the prep nurse smells smoke on me she becomes angry. Don't you know it's stupid to smoke before a procedure in which you're about to be put down, she says. Oh, I say. What's wrong with your hands, she says, picking up one and looking at its scars. When my hand lands again by my side I realize it is shaking.

Next thing, eyes open, Dr. Moss above. He says my name. I hear him. He says it again. I still hear him. He says it again and I say: what. Thata girl, he says. He speaks slow and loud, THE SUR GER Y IS O VER THERE WAS A COMP LI CA TION

After six days in ICU I am taken to a regular floor where people have all kinds of things wrong with them. I do not have a roommate, thank Jesus. The operation aggravated the internal bleeding and my lipase and amylase levels have not improved, but have become worse. My blood pressure is no longer low, but now my pulse is too rapid. I have developed a serious kidney infection. There is nothing to do but wait and take antibiotics and blood clotting drugs plus morphine for pain. I cannot eat food and am not to put ice chips on my tongue since anything activates enzymes gone wild which are already attacking everything as food and digesting it anyway.

Eventually veins blow in hands, arm, and ankles, and the iv is put in my chest. I cannot watch television since I become hysterical when I see Taco Bell commercials. Even though a drip gives nourishment I still feel hunger. There is nothing to do but lie there and cry. Nice Day Nurse Shirley says that's normal after surgery plus the morphine and there you go. At the end of the first week I do something amazing. I cry nine hours straight. Even Cruel Day Nurse Betty feels bad about it, touches my head, coos. When I finally stop, I ask myself why, why did I cry and why did I stop. Two questions with the same answer. But it isn't an answer. Not really, since she was never an answer but still, she was my mother.

* * *

My sister visits days she's not working. Nurses check on me and Giant Orderly Jenny fetches me to walk around the unit for exercise. Giant Orderly Jenny likes to talk so these walks can take in excess of an hour. She talks about Bob who goes to her church. Giant Orderly Jenny seems to go to church constantly but only ever talks about Bob. Bob works at the bank but is doing a long-distance certificate course in interior design. He wears bright suits, like grass green or peach ones, with printed kerchiefs made to match. I don't tell her I think Bob is probably gay. How is Bob today, I ask Giant Orderly Jenny. She giggles like a schoolgirl. Honey, let me tell you.

The pain is constant. They take me off morphine since it's messing up my veins and put me on a drug cocktail they give as a shot twice a day. My enzyme levels do not improve so I still cannot eat. I cannot leave the hospital until I can eat by myself.

When not trying to convince my sister she is going to be a mother, having sexual dreams about food, and taking walks, I read Tolstoy. If he were a car he'd be a Cadillac. Which, I find out, is the kind of car Bob drives.

Hello Ginger Rogers.

The voice is female but the body male. The only time I've heard a voice like that it belonged to a drag queen. It's a voice like a Hoover, strangely velvety and deep but shot through with estrogen.

Charlie is the night nurse. I do not know why when he makes his rounds between two and four in the morning this must include waking me. At first it really bugs the shit out of me but he's so nice I eventually let it drop.

Then it occurs to me that I like him. He asks how I'm feeling like he wants to know. I begin to look forward to seeing Charlie in a weird way. After he gives me the once-over, cleans my surgical wounds, and checks the machines, sometimes he sticks around to talk.

He wakes me by placing his hand on my arm and gently rocking it back and forth until my eyes open. There is Charlie, glowing in the room's dim light. Sometimes he doesn't wake me by rocking my arm back and forth because I spontaneously open my eyes to find him standing there, smiling. I was just about to wake you, he says.

My sister has a new boyfriend, Ron. Ron is a yoga instructor she met at the grocery store. Standing by the apples he told her gentle yoga was great for pregnant moms and gave her his card. Because he looked like the guitar player in Aerosmith she decided to set up an appointment during which they fell in love. Ron isn't freaked out my sister is pregnant because pregnant women are beautiful "gateways." I ask my sister if Ron wants to be a father. Totally, she says, he is so into it. He wants to save the placenta and do an ancient tree ceremony. What's a placenta ancient tree ceremony, I ask. It's when you connect human and tree life forces, she says.

I ask my sister about my father even though we have different fathers and didn't know either of them. My father split when I was three to work offshore in Miami and no one ever heard from him again. Do you think that's weird, I ask my sister. What, do you mean like it's bullshit? I don't know, she says, at least yours went somewhere cool. Mine just went to Tennessee.

*   *   *

Hello Ginger Rogers.

Charlie opens my gown and examines my stitches. How are they healing, I ask. Well, he says, they could be better. He puts on gloves and pulls out the iodine and swabs.

You can get better, he says, you know there's nothing you can't do if you set your mind to it. I can think of some things, I say. Well you wrote that long paper in Scotland didn't you? I guess, I say. Of course you did, he says. How did you do that?

I did it like my favorite object, the kind that can be opened in which you find another like it within it but smaller which you open to find another like it within it but smaller which you open to find another like it within it but smaller, I say. I repeated myself.

Ahh, Charlie says, that kind of object. The indulgence in simultaneous hope and disappointment. The question of what it will lead to next insinuates there will be something.

Yes, I say. But meanwhile the object inwardly reprojects and though there are trick-flash hellos of a possible something they are emptied again into nothing.

But in the end it gives something, he says. It is the last thing opened and within it another like it but smaller being so small it cannot contain a version of itself to be opened. The opening is too small to see. There is only a nub. But that's something.

I guess that's the part I don't like, I say. The nub part.

Why not, he says.

Because the ability to recognize quits and the nub is what the awful condition looks like.

Yes, he says. Recognition ceasing, all your methods useless, how will you proceed at the end of being known?

I don't know, I say. That's it exactly.

Have you ever thought, he says, to use the nub. Apply to paper and rub. The imposter you that you have written in.

He closes my gown and tucks the blankets. I guess I hadn't thought of that, I say. He pulls off the gloves and tosses them toward the trashcan and misses. Damn, he says. Good-night Ginger Rogers.

* * *

I tell myself a story.

Barbecued pigeons on power lines tangle every corner pulsing dry electric. I tell myself the saddest story = the one you tell yourself.

Tell myself in the stall, hogs and dolls. I tell a winter one in moonlight. Tell the story, Ginger Rogers, to the story path's runway.

Then run down it. Dead crowds cheer.

My sister says, Do you know that shitty feeling you get when you think about someone major involved in something horrible or totally fucked up? Yes, I say. Well remember Rod. I remembered Rod. The boyfriend of her gothic period.

Today I was triggered there I was boom but I said no I'm gonna go with it, I'm gonna adjust the frequency, I'm gonna Be Here Now. The way you do it is you let the triggered vibration in by imagining it as a present you're giving to your heart then your heart gives you a present. It gives you a feeling. Wow, I say.

Yeah, she says, then Ron and I took the letters Rod wrote me, death slash sex stuff, very dark, very, and burned them on the grill. Not mine I don't own one but the neighbor's who I share the deck with.

Lying in bed looking at my sister in her pastel hemp yoga jumper eating nuts and seeds in the lotus position in a hospital chair, I know the shitty feeling. I am reminded of the wet wool blanket that suffocated a baby in our town the year I was eight. The baby suffocated in a wool blanket that had been soaking in mop water.

Hello Ginger Rogers.

You looked like you were dreaming, he says.
I was, I say. About what, he says.
A man, I say.
A special someone?
Well, that's one way to put it.

Surely a girl like you has a special someone.
I used to.

Was he in the dream?
No, I say. The dream was about a man, but also men.
Sometimes one man made of the parts of many men.
What kind of men?
The wrong kind, I say.

What happens in the dream?
I sleep with the man, which is the same as sleeping with
all the men he is made of.
Do you love these men?
I do not love these men.
Odd, he says, because in other areas of your life you are
sincere.

I want to, I say. I imagine scenarios. But I never really do.
I do something close, I see them.
Do you dream this dream often?
Yes, I say.

Charlie takes off the gloves and tosses them toward the wastebasket. One misses. He picks it up and puts it in his pocket. Does the man in your dream stand for someone? I don't know, I say. Well, he says, he stands in for something.

He understands dark and complex women, I say.
Yes, he says, he knows what you need.
But, he says, when you eventually remember why you really slept with him a longing is in place. At first the longing is to be wanted against your slipping visage in his daily life.

I don't want him, I say.
No, he says. What you want is for him to want you. When his wanting ends, it returns you to yourself.

I want to delay that, I say.
Yes, he says. The imminent suffering within the present moment is difficult. And too, you want to be wanted in so much as everybody does. Well, he says, maybe more than some people.

Maybe the sex makes it worth it, I say.

The sex is graphic, he says.

He is a bad man, I say.

Yes, he says, because when he said he was a bad man you were looking in his eyes and it made you cold inside when he smiled.

He wasn't smiling because it was funny, I say.

No, he says, he was smiling like the devil.

You know, he says, if there's one thing I've learned working at the hospital it's this: if he says he's a son of a bitch he probably isn't lying. On that note good-night.

Good-night what, I say.

Ginger Rogers, he says.

＊　＊　＊

I thought of you as Giant Orderly Jenny spoke. Her mouth moving, soundless. All the sounds turned down. *Perspective.* The upper exalt. Your rib bones rippled. You held ankles flush. Upper exalt in door crack light held ankles flush. To a sweating face. You upper exalt in door light. Held ankles flush to a sweating face. Hamstrings busting ((stone eggs knock)) sweating scarlet sweating.

* * *

Hello Ginger Rogers.

Why do you call me that, I say. Don't you like the movies, he says. Yes, I say, I used to want to be in the movies. Charlie undoes the surgical tape and pulls back the bandage. I saw myself in the mirror today, I say. Oh yeah, he says. Anyway, I say, I don't look like Ginger Rogers.

Looking pretty good tonight, he says. He pops off his gloves and aims for the trashcan. The gloves land on the rim. He's improving.

At the door he turns and says, One day you'll be glad you didn't go into the movie business. You think so, I say. I know so, he says.

The business of sweethearts is a lonely business.

And what was it you thought while looking in the mirror?

I thought it was sharp so shaped as to cut——acutely perceptive; extremely sensitive, great acumen; astute, animated by desire, biting, wonderful; marvelous, keen. That it was pertaining to the mind, of, pertaining to, or affected by a disorder of the mind, performed by or existing in the mind.

I thought to undergo a penalty, to undergo, be subjected to, or endure anything——is like a state of extreme necessity. A state of an airplane, requiring immediate assistance, as when on fire. As well there was——the act of losing possession. Deprivation from separation, something lost; as a relation, terminating in an edge, not blunt. It bore a tone. Raised a chromatic half-step in pitch. I thought, well if that isn't a medium-length all purpose sewing needle.

Sudden, instances of this grief.

Extra special news alert! Nice Day Nurse Shirley says as she enters the room. Your blood work came back and today you can have some Jell-O! When, I say, when can I have the Jell-O? Lunchtime, Nice Day Nurse Shirley says. When is lunchtime, I say. In a half hour! Will it be red or green, I say. I don't know, she says, sometimes it's even orange or yellow!

I call my sister. Get your ass over here I'm eating Jell-O. My sister comes and brings Morty from work. A few minutes later Ron bursts through the door. Blessed be! he says. Giant Orderly Jenny opens the door and ceremoniously enters with a lunch cart. On top of the cart is Jell-O in a plastic cup. Look at that, says Nice Day Nurse Shirley, it's green!

Gosh, I say, this is so exciting. Are you ready? Nice Day Nurse Shirley says. Ready! I say. I slide the spoon in the Jell-O. The Jell-O warbles and reflects sunlight streaming in from the window. Ron begins to chant. Ron, I say, you're going to have to stop that. My sister shoots me a hurt look. I mean, I say, could you please do that inside your head. Sure, Ron says, you bet.

I raise the spoon to my trembling lips and put the Jell-O in my mouth. It dissolves as sugary water. I do it again and again until the Jell-O is gone. With each bite I feel strength return. I have never been so happy, I say. Really, I mean I am really happy. Everyone is gathered around the bed smiling and clapping. Giant Orderly Jenny looks like she might cry. I have been in the hospital for six weeks and it is the first time I have taken food other than intravenously.

I'd like to take this opportunity to thank everyone, I say. Everyone says it's nothing. No really, I say, you're all terrific. We love you, Ron says. It's special you were all here for this, it means a lot everyone got to be here, except for Night Nurse Charlie. I wish Night Nurse Charlie could've been here. Who's that? says Nice Day Nurse Shirley.

A woman in a navy blue suit with a TV commercial voice sits across from my bed. She smells like hand sanitizer. Dr. Moss says you get to go home in a couple of days. Right, I say. Hey that's just great, she says. Mind if I ask you a couple of questions. Before I can answer she says, Hey great.

Can you give me a description of the gentleman who came to your room. And how many times would you say he came to your room. Do you know what time. You said he "checked" your drips and attended your surgical wounds, did he put anything in your drips. No, are you sure. You mentioned he spoke to you, did he reveal personal details, did he perform any . . . exams. Hey that's just great O.K. bye-bye.

No one will tell me what is going on. I ask Nice Day Nurse Shirley but she says she doesn't know and even if she did there is a policy that prevents her from speaking to patients about official hospital business. I ask Giant Orderly Jenny about it during our last walk together. Honey I don't know, she says, but I have a guess. I guess he was a janitor or something. Yeah, I say, I guess he was.

The Life of Ginger Rogers, by Ginger Rogers

FTER THE HOSPITAL I MOVE INTO THE ONE-
room apartment above Ron's garage. My sister
has moved in with Ron and has also become
his secretary. This means she schedules his yoga
appointments and bakes wheat-free cookies for his
weekly Truth-In-Bliss meetings. They painted Ron's dining room purple for the purpose of these meetings and
different people take turns sitting in the middle of the
floor on a velour cushion while other members of the
group shoot x-ray vibes of love into the person and tell
them their wounded inner child is beautiful. Though I
find it petty that when feeling vulnerable Ron must
"white-light himself because of my identification illu-
sions based on emotional poverty," basically we all get
along. The most important thing is that he loves my sister and her unborn baby who he will legally adopt after
the pagan handfasting ceremony.

Sitting around one afternoon taking bong hits while my
sister bakes wheat-free cookies, Ron tells me they've
decided to name the baby Ganesha after the Hindu ele-
phant god of fortune. I tell him I do not think it is a good
idea to name a kid something like that because it may end

up ironic, after which he tells me he and my sister love me very much even though my heart chakra is blocked and probably always will be. As he loads another bowl I say, Thanks Ron. You bet, he says.

Movies are mostly stupid, Ron says. I suppose so, I say.
Didn't you think up one in the hospital? my sister asks.
Yeah, I say, I sure did.

Screenplay: *The Internal Committee Meeting*

Cast of Characters: The Blue Lagoon People, The Butcher, Jacques Derrida, The Knight Antonius Block, Rembrandt, Death, Ginger Rogers.

Setting: *As the scene begins the Knight Antonius Block is holding a crucifix—a relic from his time in the Crusades. He paces the length of a nondescript room. The rest of the Internal Committee members sit around a large table. It is hot. An old iron fan offers little relief. It whirs. Rembrandt, distracted, taps a paintbrush on the table. Ginger Rogers slouches in a chair, fanning herself with a feather boa while smoking a cigarette. The Butcher, donning a bloody apron, is pouring a scotch. He hands it to Ginger Rogers, then pours himself one. Jacques Derrida closes the book he is reading while eyeing the scotch Ginger Rogers is holding. The Blue Lagoon people [Brooke Shields and a Blond Guy] wear furry, minimal clothing and make grooming gestures toward one another. Suddenly a clock [out of view] strikes. The Knight Antonius Block sits down at the table.*

THE KNIGHT ANTONIUS BLOCK: The bell bellows in the distance. REMBRANDT: We are unaided in our ability to dispense with the desire to follow. GINGER ROGERS: A flaming want to tag along. THE BUTCHER: Any alternative would do. THE BLUE LAGOON PEOPLE [in unison]: I wish I could go with you.

DEATH: But don't you like it here? THE KNIGHT ANTONIUS BLOCK: Well, it's O.K. JACQUES DERRIDA: L'etre et le neante. Les mots. GINGER ROGERS: Who's that guy? THE BUTCHER: I don't know so let's ignore him.

THE KNIGHT ANTONIUS BLOCK: You don't even know what I'm talking about. REMBRANDT: I don't care, I'd like to talk nineteen to the dozen anyway. GINGER ROGERS: I want to prattle. THE BUTCHER: Everybody over there wants to prattle over here.

THE KNIGHT ANTONIUS BLOCK: You can just rankle and flake here. DEATH: If it's flaking you want, you can do it here or there. REMBRANDT: Redirect, make a clean breast of it. GINGER ROGERS: Where was I going when I was going to go? THE BUTCHER: I don't like your kind, Chief.

DEATH: So what. You can't get rid of me. REMBRANDT: I suspect death will be exactly as I imagine it. THE BLUE LAGOON PEOPLE: I hope we are rescued. THE KNIGHT ANTONIUS BLOCK: I have seen many footstep death by use of the grossest means.

REMBRANDT: The last five minutes is the most important part. GINGER ROGERS: But I would like to have more than just one lousy flare. THE BUTCHER: Doubly the raison d'être to luxuriate in what is contracted. THE KNIGHT ANTONIUS BLOCK: What happens in the last five minutes? REMBRANDT: I forgot.

GINGER ROGERS: Remember that as luck would have it, Lady was her name. THE BUTCHER: But how long does this last? DEATH: Not long at all. JACQUES DERRIDA: Le Diable et le Bon Dieu. THE BLUE LAGOON PEOPLE: Will he ever shut up? He seems angry or dead.

THE KNIGHT ANTONIUS BLOCK: You'd be too if you died in the French Revolution. THE BUTCHER: Not exactly "a day out." GINGER ROGERS: To the dreadful edge. THE BUTCHER: What is beyond the edge?

DEATH: They say a flat black sea. THE KNIGHT ANTONIUS BLOCK: They say the sea turns into a sheet of fire. REMBRANDT: They say that within are terrible, merciless creatures. GINGER ROGERS: Then an edge you fall off of. THE BUTCHER: Then what?

DEATH: They say nothing. THE KNIGHT ANTONIUS BLOCK: I thought it would be different. DEATH: It turned out not so at all. THE BUTCHER: I fold. GINGER ROGERS: I peer. THE BLUE LAGOON PEOPLE: We ate of the poisonous red berries. DEATH: The End.

That is a terrible idea for a movie, Ron says. It isn't entertaining. I don't know, my sister says, that guy from *The Blue Lagoon* was really hot. O.K., well Really Hot doesn't mean it's a good movie, Ron says. My sister pouts. Ron looks out the window with a mystical and sad look on his face.

Why does it have to be entertaining? I ask. You can't expect people to pay ten bucks for something that is going to make them feel weird or awful, Ron says. What we need, Ron says, is light. We need light in this world, not more darkness.

It's not like I actually think this is a real movie or anything but it bothers me. I don't want to choose between light or dark. I think there is a third choice. It includes light and dark but is not limited to either. It's both and more.

I take a job restoring antiques down the street at this guy Dean's. Dean doesn't actually restore antiques, but ruins them. Because he's the only guy around who works on old stuff he gets jobs nonetheless. In his shop there are many labeled drawers containing tools. One of the drawers is labeled PORNOGRAPHY and when you open it there is a newspaper clipping of a picture of high school cheerleaders with a caption that reads, *Go Tigers!* Dean didn't care about my lack of restoration knowledge. What mattered was my astrological sign and if I smoked dope. It turns out being a dope-smoking Air sign is ideal for working in the restoration business.

Dean smokes shitty dope out of pipes he makes from screwing together various tubes, nuts, and bolts. Dean is also a speed freak. He gets speed along with a bunch of other stuff from his psychiatrist. Every day he asks if I want speed and every day I say no.

As far as jobs go it's a joke but I get paid and sometimes I really like working on the old stuff. For the most part I work while Dean rattles on about conspiracy theories, ice skaters, or his favorite topic, JonBenet Ramsey, who he is unnaturally obsessed with.

Strange things you do, you now know. So plan a walk, resolve to do it, begin. To interpret one side of your brain. Exercise, Nourishment, Plan a walk, Resolve to do it, Begin. One side sends a mission to the other side. The Things You Do list forms. Exercise Nourishment. Plan Resolve Begin. You notice. A forlorn list. Exercise Nourishment Plan a walk Resolve Begin. You forgot. Oh you think, remember. Exercise, nourishment, plan a walk, resolve to do it, begin. If I happen upon this list it is because I have achieved mission control. Exercise Nourishment Walk Begin. You are always doing one thing on the other, contraband list, but over time that list changed. It use to be: bang, blood, and drain. It was worse then. Exercise Nourishment. Plan a walk, Resolve to do it. Begin.

Dean talks about my position at the shop in a long-term way. He says I should take initiative and establish "shop goals," which is pointless since who would meet them and for what reason.

Dean has a kid unimaginatively named Sonny who lives in Florida and works at a tuxedo rental shop in the mall. He says Sonny is one of the special people, born that way, star quality, charisma, but people like us, we're ants, we can't all be stars or the night would be as bright as day. This is Dean's way of trying to sell me on the idea of setting shop goals. Like if I accept that I can't be as special as Sonny I'll find my place in the scheme of things, which is what I should try and do.

I don't know what I'm doing. It's liberating and depressing. I could move to Hawaii, but once there what would I do? I've got to come up with a plan.

What are you doing, my sister says as I haul an archaic piece of junk into her kitchen. I'm gonna wipe this down, I say. Oh, she says, Where did it come from? A pawnshop, I say. What is it, she says. It's a word processor, I say. What are you gonna do with it, she says. I was thinking while I sort things out it would come in handy, I say. Are you gonna type job applications with it? No, I say, I thought I'd write a novel. Oh, she says. What's it about? I don't know, I say. Do you know how to write a novel? No, I say, I don't.

Later I put it on the table in my garage apartment and look at it. The E, S, and N letters have been rubbed off the keyboard from use. When night comes I sit in front of it. I could write anything. How odd. But what I write is

Listen

Notes

Section titles in *I: Headbanger's Ball* are lyrics, taken in part, from the following songs:

"Hostage of This Nameless Feeling" is from "The Frayed Ends of Sanity" by Metallica.

"Get Off Your High Horse and Come to the Party" is from "Invisible" by Anthrax.

"Make a Joke and I Will Sigh and You Will Laugh and I Will Cry" is from "Paranoid" by Black Sabbath.

"This May Hurt a Little but It's Something You'll Get Used To" is from "Stinkfist" by Tool.

"Rock Hard, Ride Free" is from "Rock Hard, Ride Free" by Judas Priest.

"Run to the Hills, Run for Your Lives" is from "Run to the Hills" by Iron Maiden.

"From the Inside Out It All Looks the Same" is from "King Size" by Anthrax.

"Darling, Do You Wear the Mark" is from "Do You Wear the Mark" by Danzig.

"Crazy but That's How It Goes" is from "Crazy Train" by Ozzy Osbourne.

"Master, Master Where's the Dreams I've Been After" is from "Master of Puppets" by Metallica.

"The Only Good Indians Are Tame" is from "Run to the Hills" by Iron Maiden.

Section titles in *III: The Slaughterhouses of Glasgow* have been taken from the following sources:

"Sojourning in a Foreign Land Threshed With Guts" is from *Unknowne Land* by Eléna Rivera [Kelsey St. Press].

"Here, This Speck and This Speck You Missed" is from *Commons* by Myung Mi Kim [University of California Press].

"And Suddenly I Thought: This Is What It Means to Make a Movie in Sweden" is a quote from Ingmar Bergman in *Four Screenplays of Ingmar Bergman* [Simon & Schuster].

"Aboard, My Love! The Sun Is a Profound Gamble: Another Day and Still Another" is from *The Book of Questions,* by Edmond Jabés [translated by Rosmarie Waldrop, Wesleyan University Press].

"There Is a Host in Ghost" *is from O, Vozque Pulp* by Carlos M. Luis & Derek White [Calamari Press].

ADDITIONAL NOTES

The text in "Screenplay: The Internal Committee Meeting" in The Life of Ginger Rogers, by Ginger Rogers was greatly influenced by the photographs in "Hope & Fear / Photo-Essay, Series Two" presented by Bushwick Farms representatives Stewart Solzberg and Tara Cuthbert. The text in French are titles of works by Jean-Paul Sartre.

The "Love Song" on page 86 is from *Earth Prayers* [Harper San Francisco].

The quote on page 103 is from *The Scarlet Letter* by Nathaniel Hawthorne.

The verse on page 175 is from W.H. Auden's "In Memory of W.B. Yeats."

Part of the sentence on page 189 ["….how will you proceed at the end of being known?] comes from and genuflects to Michael Klein's book, *The End of Being Known* [The University of Wisconsin Press].

Acknowledgments

Thank you Chris Fischbach, and thanks to all the wonderful folks at Coffee House Press.

I am also indebted to The MacDowell colony, which made time and space for work possible.

For encouragement and close readings, with great affection, I thank Tama Baldwin, Helen Humphries, Joan Fiset, Christian Peet, and Jessica Godino.

Thanks to friends and colleagues who offered valuable insights into this work: Laird Hunt, Lucy Anderton-Fox, Joe DeGross, Elizabeth Rollins, Julianna Spallholz, Brad Land, Michael Boyko, and Elena Georgiou. For that plus dirty jokes and Yeats, Robert Anasi.

For many and consistent generosities I thank: Guenevere Seastrom, Kim Duckett and the "circle sisters," Mindy Gates, Zach Gates, David Lowe, Kevin Rabas, Jeff Hemphill, Sandra DeGross, Kelly Stephenson, Eléna Rivera, Richard Grant, Dawn Paul, Braden Russell, Stewart Solzberg, Tara Cuthbert, Ellen Orleans, Denise Sadler, Cynthia Ona Innis, Greg Isles, and Rosemary and Charles Hall. My sincere gratitude also goes to Roger and Anna Saterstrom, George Haymans, and my parents, Ann Coleman, and Hugh and Karen Redhead.

I would like to thank Sequoyah Christine Rich and Shannon Poposhill for their generosity of spirit and for the contributions their work makes to the field of trauma therapy. Finally, thanks to Hannah and Tia. Where ever you each may be.

I also am grateful to the many people who shared with me their private, difficult stories of the body during the course of this project.

Funder Acknowledgments

Coffee House Press is an independent nonprofit literary publisher. Our books are made possible through the generous support of grants and gifts from many foundations, corporate giving programs, individuals, and through state and federal support. Coffee House Press receives general operating support from the Minnesota State Arts Board, through an appropriation by the Minnesota State Legislature and from the National Endowment for the Arts, and major general operating support from the McKnight Foundation, and from the Target Foundation. Coffee House also receives support from: an anonymous donor; the Elmer and Eleanor Andersen Foundation; the Buuck Family Foundation; the Patrick and Aimee Butler Family Foundation; Stephen and Isabel Keating; the Lenfesty Family Foundation; Rebecca Rand; the law firm of Schwegman, Lundberg, Woessner & Kluth, P.A.; the James R. Thorpe Foundation; the Woessner Freeman Family Foundation; Wood-Rill Foundation; and many other generous individual donors.

This activity is made possible in part by a grant from the Minnesota State Arts Board, through an appropriation by the Minnesota State Legislature and a grant from the National Endowment for the Arts. MINNESOTA STATE ARTS BOARD

 TARGET.

To you and our many readers across the country, we send our thanks for your continuing support.

Good books are brewing at coffeehousepress.org

Selah Saterstrom is the author of three novels, *Slab, The Meat and Spirit Plan,* and *The Pink Institution,* all published by Coffee House Press. Widely published and anthologized, she also curates Madame Harriette Presents, an occasional series. She teaches and lectures across the United States and is the director of creative writing at the University of Denver.

C O L O P H O N

The Meat and Spirit Plan was designed at Coffee House Press,
in the historic warehouse district of downtown Minneapolis.
The type is set in Perpetua.